PROPERTY OF
FOX RUN AT ORCHARD PARK
One Fox Run Lane
Orchard Park, New York 14127
(716) 662-5001

SARAH CLARKSON:
Harlot Nurse of the Civil War

The secret diary of a lusty nurse in a time of war

A NOVEL BY
RONALD ARONDS

Palmetto Publishing Group
Charleston, SC

Sarah Clarkson: Harlot Nurse of the Civil War
Copyright © 2020 by Ronald Arouds

All rights reserved

No portion of this book may be reproduced, stored in a retrieval system, or transmitted in any form by any means—electronic, mechanical, photocopy, recording, or other—except for brief quotations in printed reviews, without prior permission of the author.

First Edition

Printed in the United States

Hardcover: 978-1-64990-004-3
Paperback: 978-1-64990-003-6
eBook: 978-1-64990-005-0

INTRODUCTION

Those whose names live on in history have the myths of their lives passed on as the one and only truth, solid and unwavering. Even future historians have difficulty finding new information with which to break through the myth.

However, once in a great while, a document, a page, a sentence, a fragment arises which sheds light upon the generally accepted truth creates a crack, no matter how small, in the myth. Yet once in a hundred years or more a secret is unearthed which changes our view of the historical figure forever.

While spending a sunny summer afternoon in a suburban New Jersey community garage sailing as I was often wont to do to pass the time I found myself pawing through the usual brick a brack and moldy old records. In the bottom of a box of old "Archie" comics I felt something odd. It was a slender booklet with the word Diary written on the front in faded gold leaf letters. It seemed out of place among the adventures of Archie and his chums, and at first I thought of tossing it aside. But stopping myself I decided to keep it after all, to use it as a notepad for any telephone messages I might need to take in the future. I paid the $3.50 for the whole box and then went home to enjoy hours of fun reading the antics of Jughead Jones and Big Moose as well as the somewhat salacious scampering about of Archie's women, Betty and Veronica.

It was indeed an enjoyable passing of the time. By the time I reached the bottom of the box of comics I came once more upon the aged diary book. As I removed it from the box I noticed that there was writing on the pages of the diary. What a waste of money, I thought. A used diary – I couldn't even use it to take phone messages. But still the afternoon was not yet waning, so having finished with my Archies I decided to read the ancient looking script between the covers of the moldering volume.

What was there is what is now in this book. The nurse of long ago, the founder of the international nursing and charitable organization known to all in the civilized world, The Healing Bosom Nursing Society. Yes, this was in fact the diary of the one and only Sarah Clarkson, the iconic figure whose name alone brings forth visions of selfless healing of those in need.

Shakespeare said that some people are born great, some people achieve greatness, and some people have greatness thrust upon them. This diary adds a new part to those Shakespearean words, that is that some people have greatness thrust into them. This then dear reader is the secret diary of Sarah Clarkson.

Ronald Arouds

This is the diary of Sarah Clarkson, to be returned if lost to Shippensburg, New Jersey

August 1, 1860

Dear Diary,

Another miserable day in the muggy heat of the wildernesses of southern New Jersey. Summer is coming to an end. I dread the thought. To have to return to the unrewarding life of a spinster school teacher gives me the shivers, as if I had the ague. I get no respect from the mothers of the rotten snot nosed little urchins I have forced upon me each school year. Each of the mothers is convinced that their child is the modern day incarnation of the gods of old. Far be it for me to give them a rude awakening, that in fact each child is as dull as the next. I yearn to be free of this existence, but where could a thirty year old unmarried woman go in these days? It appears that my fate is to live with my parents and help raise others children for the rest of my days on Earth.

October 3, 1860

Dear diary,

I find my self becoming lonelier by the hour. All of my little playmates of my youth have grown into haggard old women. I have nobody to share my thoughts with except for you dear diary. The men of this dreadful part of the world are either drunken married men or simpering, foppish dandies. Why are there no manly men, strong, sweaty, muscular men who take what they want without asking permission?

At night I listen to my father and mother from their room down the hallway. After a night of hard drinking with the other men of the town, my father returns home and fairly rips off mother's bodice. She runs from him, but he follows her as she tries to hide under the covers of their bed. She is no match for his desires, and before long I hear the moaning of my mother, the rocking of their bed, and the deep grunting sound of my father. These nightly sounds have a strange effect on me. Without consciously being aware, I find my hand drifting beneath my night clothes and gently rubbing in my special woman's spot between my thighs. The feeling is one of indescribable pleasure. I dream of being swept up in a man's strong arms. I would not run from him as mother does. No, I would spend my days satisfying his lustful desires.

December 10, 1860

Dear diary,

War is declared! Mr. Lincoln has called for volunteers to force the southern states to remain in our glorious union. Although he is homely, Mr. Lincoln has an erect posture, a firmness not found in many men. He has a tall stiff look about him. He is long, but with a thickness all around. His head is large and prominent. I feel myself strangely aroused, my breath growing short, an odd moistness dampening my undergarments, when I gaze upon his lithograph in the newspapers. I feel certain that he will be the one to spray his rigid powerful hose upon the burning flames ignited by the rebellious southerners and so cool their ardor.

July 5, 1861

Dear Diary,

I can stand it no longer. The southerners won't be subdued despite the gallant efforts of our soldiers. I have achieved nothing in this another school year. The children seem to become stupider with every new term. How can I sit still while the events of the century unfold. I read of them in the newspapers but I yearn to see history being made on my own.

Just yesterday there was the first true battle of the war at a small creek in Virginia rather foolishly named Bull Run. The stories tell of the brave sacrifices of our northern troops, but I interpret this to mean that the southerners have won a great victory. It is feared that they will next march on Washington.

I have decided. I will travel south to give succor to our wounded men. I will sneak away tonight while my father is asleep in a drunken stupor and mother recovers from his nightly assaults.

July 26, 1861

Dear Diary,

I have arrived at our camp at Spottsylvania in Northern Virginia. I was able to gain passage through the lines by creating a story of how I was an experienced nurse and that it was my duty as a loyal American to provide relief to our wounded men. Of course dear diary you must keep my secret – I have never had one minute of nursing training in all of my life!

The trip itself was quite eventful. I hired a coachman in the dark of night to take me to the bottom of my former state, New Jersey at the city of Cape May. The entire trip the coachman inquisitively asked about why a young woman all alone would b e traveling so far. At one point he claimed that his horses were tired, and that he and I should share a room at the local tavern for the rest of the evening. I declined his offer, and for a reason I don't understand he became somewhat agitated. He persisted in his entreaties, at one point offering to refund the fee he had charged me for our midnight trip. I politely declined. After all, I was on my way to the battle front.

By dawn we had arrived. The coachman seemed quite unhappy when we reached our destination. He suggested that I must be tired from our long night time trip, and that perhaps we should rest in a room at the Cape May Hotel for a bit since the ferry boat to Delaware would not arrive several hours. I thanked him for his offer, but instead decided to visit the sites of the city. Compared to Shippensburg, Cape May is a metropolis! The coachman continued to mutter under his breath as we parted.

The city was fascinating to a simple country girl like myself. The storefronts filled with their fine clothing and sweet pastries nearly overwhelmed me.

And the people were so polite! At every new street I was approached by the most handsome men, offering to escort me around the town, or to come back to their homes for a fresh meal. I was quite hungry, and it was several more hours before my transport arrived, so I accepted the offer of a tall gentleman in a top hat to come to his home for a brief afternoon repose.

When we arrived his serving lady brought us a warm lunch. I don't know why, but I had the distinct feeling that this servant was looking at me slyly, a squinting of her eyes and a small smile on her lips until she finally retired from the sitting room where my gentleman and I were eating. She locked the door behind us once she left.

The meal was warm and quite satisfying, but dear diary I must say that the atmosphere in the sitting room became quite heated as well. I felt myself swooning. As I began to grow faint my gentleman quickly came to my side and grabbed me in his strong arms. I opened my eyes to see a look that can only be described as one of passion on his face. Up to that point I had only read of such a thing in the secret books I kept hidden under my mattress but now I saw what was previously just words on a page. I parted my lips slightly in surprise. My gentleman brought his lips to mine. I could feel my face turn red. I heard myself give off a slight moan as he kept his lips held tightly against mine. I was thirty years old and this was my first kiss. It was everything I had dreamed it would be.

The afternoon was too short. I almost considered waiting until the next day to continue my trip to Virginia. My gentleman removed his top hat. He pulled my body closer to his. My bosom pressed against his chest, giving me that same strange feeling between my thighs that I would get while lying alone in my bed back home. We kissed and kissed until I felt I would be able to breath no longer. The lack of air put me into a dream like state, one that I would remember forever and that I would continually seek for the rest of my days. I had read in my secret books about men who had taken opium and so would bring a feeling of joy unlike any that could be felt in the earthly world. I imagined that this feeling was like my opium.

Sadly, we had to part. We rushed to the dock in just enough time for my trip across the Delaware Bay. My gentleman grasped my hand and made me promise to visit him when I passed through Cape May again. It was a promise I eagerly made. A kiss is something that a woman only does in the privacy of a gentleman's chamber. Instead we gazed into each others eyes knowingly one last time before I boarded the ferry boat.

July 31, 1861

Dear Diary,

I have arrived in Virginia after my long trip. The boat ride across the Delaware Bay was somewhat rough, the water swelling as we plunged deep into the Bay. The glow I felt after my interlude with my gentleman must still have shown as many a man on the ferry came to me to ask after my health. I assured them that the redness of my face was simply caused by this being my first boat ride. They all offered to sit with me below decks on the boat. I barely heard them. The thoughts of my gentleman's strong manly hands holding me, stroking me through my bodice and petticoats, pressing himself against my bosom, kissing me with his warm soft lips. I would dream of that afternoon many a time as I lay in bed at night, or on a lazy afternoon as I let my mind wander.

The trip through Delaware was rather sedate, but Maryland! As soon as I approached the border I encountered a veritable swarm of blue. Maryland I found out was a state that still held slaves, yet it also surrounded our capital and our stalwart president Mr. Lincoln. I had hoped to catch a glimpse of him, to see if he was as big, tall and erect as he appeared in the newspapers. But it was not to be.

In order to protect the president Maryland was filled with our soldiers in blue. Sentiment for the rebellion was strong in Maryland and our president was not going to allow another state to go south. I had to go through many a checkpoint before finally reaching the borders of the rebellion. At some of these checkpoints the soldiers told me that they needed to check my body for any concealed weapons or other contraband. I allowed them to rub their hands all over me. I must do whatever is necessary, whatever is required of me, to protect our beloved Union.

Virginia, the home of our presidents yet now part of a breakaway republic. But oh, the devastation! The war was less than a year old yet as far as the eye could see the land was stripped bare, denuded by the strong men of our army. I felt a swell of emotion in my breast as I looked across the land.

Oh dear diary, I have written too much for one day. It is night and my feeble candle light barely illuminates my camp tent. I can hear the sentries marching about, the sound of their boots on the ground act as a lullaby. Goodnight, dear diary. I feel that I will have the most pleasant of dreams tonight.

August 19, 1861

Dear Diary,

Virginia is so steamy and hot. My former home in New Jersey seems positively frigid by comparison. The men feel the heat as well, and when they are not on guard duty they often strip off their tunics. Oh dear diary, do you think me bad? The strong rippling muscles on the mend bodies bring forth an indescribable feeling in my bosom and loins. I know I am to tend to the wounded but I often find myself spying on the men as they work and play with their upper bodies exposed. And here is another secret dear diary that you mustn't tell a soul. There have been times when I felt it safe that I have hidden behind a bush to watch the men as they bathe in the nearby creek. I feel so naughty, but I can't seem to stop myself.

November 25, 1861

Dear Diary,

Although encamped in northern Virginia our army cannot seem to move farther south. The fighting season ended a month ago and now we go into winter quarters.

Our president the manly Mr. Lincoln, has declared a holiday of prayer and reflection to be known as Thanksgiving in support of our troops so far away from home. The soldiers chose to celebrate as well. After a perfunctory prayer session the feast began.

Although officially frowned upon, the leaders of the army understood the need for the men to relax and so each soldier was given as many a share of whiskey as he desired.

The men were all soon under the spell of the whiskey. Unlike my father who would seethe with anger after he was drunk here the whiskey seemed to bring humor to the men. Even I was offered a cup of the whiskey. At first I demurred, but with some little convincing I was persuaded. I felt a sudden warmth rush throughout my entire body. A smile passed on my lips as I felt an unexpected naughtiness enter my mind.

A fiddler began to strike up a tune and soon the men were engaged in a lively attempt at the Virginia Reel. I laughed at their awkwardness. Seeing two men dancing together was the most humorous thing I had ever seen. Without warning one of the men grabbed me around the waist and pulled me into the dance. The rest of the men gathered around and cheered as I spun to the tune. Being the only woman among a whole army of young men I soon found myself the belle of the ball. My turn, no my turn the men called out, each wishing to take their turn with me. I could tell the men who had been drinking too much of the whiskey since as we spun about they had difficulty keeping their balance. Their hands would slide down from my waist to my bottom where they would grip me tight as the rest of the men cheered even louder. One of the men was so deeply into his drunkenness that he accidentally slid his hand under my dress and gripped my uncovered bottom tightly. I let out a small squeal as he did so. The men fairly howled at that accidental sliding of the hand beneath my dress. More whiskey was offered to me. I felt lightheaded, a combination of the twirls about the dance floor and the whiskey I was most certain. Soon the men were coming to blows, each of them trying to get their turn to dance with me. One of the men grabbed me and lifted me away from the man who had slid his hand beneath my dress. Angry shouts arose as he tried to take his turn dancing with me, each man wishing to take me for a spin. I saw a flash of steel as one of the soldiers demanded his turn with me.

This Thanksgiving soiree came to an end only when the general in command of our brigade ordered the men back to their barracks under threat of imprisonment. The general looked at me with what appeared to be a confused frown. He asked if I had been harmed in any way but I assured him that the men had treated me in a respectable manner. He frowned more deeply at that. As he led me to my tent I felt myself swoon. The general carried me the rest of the way and laid me softly on my cot. I fell into a deep sleep with strange thoughts of the wild dance filling my dreams.

November 26, 1861

Dear Diary,

I feel as if I could sleep forever. My head throbbed, my feet were sore beyond words, and my mouth was as dry as the Sahara desert. Before long I noticed a loud moaning sound outside of my tent. With great irritation I threw on my shawl and opened my tent flap. I was taken aback by a seemingly endless line of men all groaning or vomiting. Please Ms. Clarkson, help us. My head hurts as if I had been shot by a rebel musket. Please use your nursing skills to end this terrible pain. I did my duty dear diary and offered the men what little comfort I could, telling them to just go back to their cots and cover their heads with a cold rag. It took the entire day, and when it was finally done I took my own advice. I don't believe I shall ever drink again.

July 2, 1862

Dear Diary,

Winter encampment ended some months ago but still our troops remained resting in their tents. After many a lazy week word arose that the rebel army was on the march again, to liberate their beloved Virginia from the army of our union.

The men were ordered to their brigades and to their surprise found themselves on the same battlefield as a year earlier, in that oddly named town of Bull Run. Finally I believed my false nursing skills would be put to the test.

And so I began my unlearned nursing dear diary. A hospital tent was erected some short distance from the field of battle. The battlefield casualties began to stream into our small hospital. Oh dear, the horror is something I shall never forget. But still, I had to do my duty.

The doctor directed me to observe a soldier who seemed dreadfully wounded in his legs, to determine if the leg must be taken off! The man lay on the stretcher with blood seeping onto his trousers from a wound in his upper leg. I steeled myself for my task as I removed his uniform and undergarments.

Diary, what I saw next astounded me. The soldiers wound was slight. But between his legs was shocking to me. I had never truly been with a man before, and even when I had spied on them as they bathed in the creek I had been too far to see the men clearly. But this! His manhood seemed to consist of a fleshy sack with a long stem of flesh connected to it. I became short of breath but managed to control myself long enough to gather my wits. I wiped the blood from his wound and prepared to place a plaster upon it to staunch the wound. But what happened next was something I had never expected. I washed him thoroughly around his upper thighs all the while keeping my eyes upon his male parts. To my shock the more I washed him the bigger his manhood grew. That it would grow at all was an amazement to me.

Oh nurse, please it hurts so. I need you to wash away the pain in my pole.

I did as he said and began to wash him all up and down his stiff pole. I believed that he was truly in pain as he moaned more and more with each washing up and down of his shaft. Suddenly he let out a deeper groan than I had ever heard and this strange liquid began to seep from the top of his staff. I didn't know what to do so I wiped it off of him. When I was done cleaning him he went back to his normal size.

Thank you nurse, You have made me forget the horror of the battlefield.

No, thank you brave soldier.

The doctor called to me - Nurse, come help. There are many other soldiers that need your assistance. I scampered to the hospital tent barely able to keep the amazement of what I had just seen a secret. If only I had another nurse to share my secrets with. But alas, it was just me the sole woman to give aid to an army of strong musky men.

July 5, 1862

Dear Diary,

Another defeat of our army as we head north again from the battlefield at Bull Run.

The battlefield casualties fairly poured in to our small hospital. I do not know why, but I felt this strong urge to remove the trousers of all the soldiers I was told to assist. Each man was different than the next, of all different sizes and even colors. I could not control myself as I gently touched each of them. Most of the men looked at me with surprise as I stroked their manhood, but I noticed that none of them complained.

Nurse, are you blind? That soldier has a wound in his shoulder, not his leg. Remove his tunic, not his trousers.

I did remove that soldier's tunic but I also kept his trousers off. Even as I staunched his wound I continued to gaze upon his thick member. As with the first soldier the more I touched him the longer he became. As with the first soldier I washed him all up and down his throbbing shaft. As with the first soldier that strange liquid issued forth from the tip of his shaft. He got off his stretcher and wandered off towards his tent. I could see him whispering to some of the other soldiers whose eyes opened wide after he spoke with them.

Nurse, nurse come here! I am in great pain and need you to help me a chorus of soldiers called.

So many wounded men and each calling to me to administer to their pain. As I approached some of the soldiers I noticed that they had already removed their trousers in order to save me the effort of doing so.

Nurse, I am wounded between my legs and need to have the blood washed away. Please nurse help me first!

I spent the rest of that long day helping as many of the men as I could, observing each one's manhood and how they differentiated from each other. I washed many a man that day.

August 1, 1862

Dear Diary,

Oh the horror that war brings to our soldiers. Nearly a month since the battle and the men still suffer from their wounds. Many of the men seem to be suffering from shell shock and not physical wounds.

As we retreated north the mens work was over until they regrouped, but my work never seemed to end. Each day a long line of soldiers waited outside of the nurses station seeking treatment for their injuries. I let them in one at a time, having each of them disrobe as they entered. I examined each one of them thoroughly, touching and rubbing their rough bodies with my soft hands. I knelt before each of the soldiers to observe their shafts. I felt as if I was a scientist doing studies on the male organ. I was fascinated at how each soldier grew at various rates and how much of their thick liquid each of them issued.

And then something even more amazing happened. As I knelt before one of the soldiers he suddenly placed his hands on each side of my head and forcibly placed his organ into my mouth. He grunted as he moved his thick shaft in and out of my mouth. I gagged on his member but at the same time felt unbelievably excited. Soon he grew even larger, as I had often noticed among the other men, and I felt the hot thickness of his liquid in my mouth. He held me tight as his liquid issued forth and so I had no choice but to drink it down. I gulped and swallowed until he let go of me. I looked up at him in amazement and he looked down at me with a sly smile on his lips.

I feel much better now nurse he said with a small snicker as he left my tent.

SEPTEMBER 3, 1862

Dear Diary,

The army is on the march again. The rebel army has entered into our sacred land at a small town in Maryland named Sharpsburg near the Antietem creek. I anxiously await the opportunity to bring relief to our big strong soldiers. The number of wounded men that arrived at my tent each day seemed to shrink as their officers ordered them to prepare for more war unless they were truly infirm. I found myself unknowingly licking my lips as I thought of the battle to come.

September 6, 1862

Dear Diary,

The battle was shocking in its ferocity. The number of wounded men was beyond description. Our troops finally have achieved a victory as the rebel army retreated back into Virginia. As a consequence we set up our field hospital in Maryland instead of following the rebels across the river.

I spent all day each day following the battle making sure our wounded soldiers were properly attended to. Some of the men were grievously wounded and were sent north to recover. It was my job to bring aid to the men who could recover and be sent back into the lines.

I did my duties with a passion. The wounded men were each made to remove their trousers, examined all over their legs and thighs by the stroking of my now experienced hands, and then granted relief from their suffering. When I would run short of water for washing their wounds I found that by first taking them into my mouth I was given an even greater ability to rapidly wash the mens shafts. This allowed me to administer to even more men each day. I knew how well their recoveries progressed since I could see a look of ecstasy on each of their faces once I had finished my work.

October 12, 1862

Dear Diary,

It seems that word of my special nursing skills has reached beyond the men of the line and into the officer's corp. I was called into our major's tent which was set off some distance from the lines of tents for the men.

Do come in Ms. Clarkson, or may I call you Sarah?

Yes please do major.

No no Sarah call me by my given name, Ambrose.

Yes Ambrose.

Sarah, I fear I do not have a spare seat for you. Supplies have been short since our great battle. Please come sit next to me on my cot.

Certainly Ambrose.

Sarah, the men speak highly of your nursing skills. Very highly in fact. I wish to make you feel as good as you make our brave men feel.

Why, whatever do you mean Ambrose? I do not understand how a man can make a woman happy since that is within the purveyance of a woman towards a man.

Oh Sarah, you silly girl. Is it possible that you have never actually been with a man despite your great deeds to our army?

The look of confusion in my eyes made him laugh softly. Come to me Sarah and let me show you the pleasure a woman can be made to feel.

Ambrose reached over to me and pulled me to him with his strong muscled grip. His hand pressed against my bosom and gave it a rough squeeze. His lips were put against mine just as my gentleman's had been before I came to aid the army but with much greater force. He was a military man so I thought he must not have had much company of a gentle woman such as myself.

Oh Ambrose, you make me swoon. I feel all warm and flush. Please Ambrose, treat me a bit more tenderly. Your soldier's grip is almost too much for me to bear.

There is a remedy for that malady Sarah. Disrobe and you shall feel the cool air against your naked creamy white flesh. You will feel a real man's touch for sure. I will not, cannot, be gentle as a woman. Only a woman could do so.

I did as he ordered and he did the same. I had seen many a man's organ during my nursing duties but with Ambrose I had no need to first bring about the growth of his shaft. He was already prepared for my nursing. I approached him with my hands outstretched.

No no Sarah, come lay with me on my cot. The pressing of our bodies against each others will bring both pleasure and warmth at the same time.

I lay on Ambrose's cot and he then lay next to me. He pulled his camp blanket over us, somewhat unnecessarily since I could already feel the same flushed and warm feeling I had felt as he pressed his hand to my bosom before. Ambrose kissed me with a passion, each new kiss giving me that wonderful feeling between my legs. I still wished for a more gentle touch.

Roll onto your back Sarah.

I did so. He climbed on to of me. My legs were still together since I did not yet know how a woman could receive pleasure from a man. With his knee he spread them apart. He reached between my legs and felt the moistness that had come there.

You are indeed ready my dear Sarah.

Oh dear diary, what happened next was truly exquisite. Just as I had used my hand and mouth to rub the wounded mens shafts so now did Ambrose use his shaft to rub inside of me. His first thrust made me gasp. Thankfully the moistness in my female region made for a smooth entry of his shaft for he was indeed well endowed, much more so than most of the hundreds of men I had seen before. The feelings he brought forth in me! Even my secret books I kept at home did not prepare me for them. My entire body responded to Ambrosia's thrusting. I thrust back, trying to bring him deeper and deeper inside of me. I howled with an indescribable delight. He laughed like a devil at my howling. Together we made an unearthly chorus. I did not know if this was the temptation of the devil or the blessings of heaven. All I knew was that I did not want it to ever stop. The blanket slid off of the rude canvas cot, exposing our naked bodies to the world. I did not care. I did not care about anything except that moment with the feeling of Ambrose's body laying against mine. I suddenly felt a thrill in my body as if the feelings I had felt between my legs in the past were magnified a thousand times over. I did not know why but my body stiffened before I went into a trance like state. No. this was not the devil's work. This feeling was truly that brought forth from the almighty himself.

Sadly I found that this, like all things in things mortal realm, could not last forever. Only heaven is infinite and I had sorely hoped that this heavenly feeling would reach to the end of time as well. The feeling though was soon a pleasant memory and when I came down from the heights of the mountain I found Ambrose lying on top of me, breathing heavily. He rolled off of me soon thereafter and I felt the chill of the air against my naked flesh for the first time.

Please cover me with your blanket Ambrose. I fear that I will be exposed to some dread disease from the cold.

Not before I gaze upon your naked beauty one more time Sarah. Roll over onto your front side so I can further see the curves of your body.

I did as he said and after he had spent many minutes gazing down upon my naked back side he covered me with his blanket. He gave me a gentle kiss.

Rest well dear Sarah. I shall return once I have called the men for inspection.

I cannot say if he had uttered anything more. Before I fell into a blissful sleep, recreating my trip to heaven in my dreams, I pondered Ambrose's words. I wonder what a soft woman's touch would feel like. I attempted to banish the thought from my mind. A woman coupling with another woman was something which would surely be impossible. But still the thought remained hidden in the recesses of my mind.

December 15, 1862

Dear Diary,

Ambrose is a wonderful lover. Each day he invites me to his tent to discuss some important issue dealing with my nursing duties yet it seems that the only nursing he wishes to discuss is how to most quickly disrobe this particular nurse. He has installed a small coal stove inside his tent to keep us warm against the unexpectedly cold Virginia weather. Not that any stove is needed. Ambrose's embrace is all that I need to keep warm. When our bodies wrestle on his cot we create such fervid energy that we have to toss his blanket aside.

Ambrose is such an experienced and worldly man. Prior to the war he was a salesman of school books for schools throughout the remotest corners of our land. We laughed about how I would not need to read my secret books if he had just come to Shippensburg to make a sale. Being a single man he found his pleasure wherever and whenever he needed to. Although our preferred method of coupling was for him to force himself onto my prone body, he has taught me other ways to make love to a man. He seems to enjoy putting his blanket on the bare ground and then have me position myself on my hands and knees like some sort off four legged animal, He grabs my hips and then thrusts into me from behind. I feel so naughty being taken like this, not even being able to see how Ambrose takes his pleasure on me. At other times he has me skewer myself on his staff. He lays on his back on his cot and then pulls me down onto him, watching my breasts swing to and fro as I ride on him as if I was riding a horse. And I do believe the analogy to be apt considering how much of a marvel the size of his staff becomes when he is aroused.

December 25, 1862

Dear Diary,

It is Christmas day. The men are melancholy in their longing for their homes. I do not feel the same. If I never set foot in Shippensburg again I will die without a regret. Ambrose has bought me a gift, some silky French undergarments he purchased from a purveyor of such scandalous items in Philadelphia. And a scandal it would be if any of the other men were to see me in this garment. It covers my bosom as if it were my second skin. When I bend over to stir the pot of coffee on his stove Ambrose never fails to comment on the roundness of my bottom partly uncovered due to the short length of the garment. I still spend most days tending to the sick men in our brigade. Sickness these days is most often a slight case of the sniffles. I believe that many of the men are faking their ailments so as to be the recipients of my special form of nursing.

Nights are spent in the tight embrace of my Ambrose. Once the sun sets and the men are in their tents I quietly sneak over to visit with Ambrose. Just as dawn is showing a hint of rising I quickly scamper back to my own cot, pretending to have slept there the night through as the morning drums awaken the troops.

December 31, 1862

Dear Diary.

Hoping to repeat the famous George Washington's stratagems, our corps commander General Johnson had decided to proceed with a surprise raid on the rebels entrenched in the town of Fredricksburg as they celebrated the New Year. Unlike the famous general Washington, our own general was distinctly lacking in military knowledge. He is what the men call a political general, one without any training or skill but who had developed bonds of friendship and family among the most influential political leaders in the land. The raid was yet another disaster. Our men were ordered to attack up an ice covered hill that was to the rear of the rebel encampment. The sound of our mens curses as they slid down these impossibly steep hill aroused the drunken rebels and quickly caused them to return to a sober state of mind. They slaughtered our men by simply firing down on them from the top of Maryes Heights were they held camp.

I did my best to bring peace to our wounded men, tending to them as I knew how best to do. I may have no formal nurses training but I did know how to bring at least a momentary joy to our men, most of whom had not felt the tender touch of a woman's hand in almost two years. Despite the cold most of the wounded men had already removed their trousers in anticipation of my brief visits to their sick beds. Such brave men need all the joy that I can give them so I made sure that each was given special attention from my healing hands. My prayers have been answered as my brave Ambrose was not in any way wounded during the failed attack. Upon his return we spent the entire night in a revelry of ecstatic love making, fearing with each day that the last trump will sound and he will be taken from my arms to his heavenly reward.

April 12, 1863

Dear Diary,

My winter revelry with my Ambrose has come to an end. Apparently one of the men, jealous of the special attention I had been giving Ambrose, pretended to feel Christian outrage as he reported our secret rendezvous up the command structure. Rather than court martial Ambrose the general billeted him in the defenses around our capital. I scarcely had a moment to bid him farewell. He could not bed me as he prepared to leave, so in order to give him a final reminder of our time in our winter idyll I knelt before him as he packed his kit bag and brought him great pleasure between my lips. The general was aware of the work I had been doing among the men, particularly after battle, and this being the fighting season he made it known that my services would most certainly soon be required.

APRIL 20, 1863

Dear Diary,

I miss Ambrose so! The warmth that his lovemaking would make me forget the horrors I have seen among our brave wounded men. By one week after he was sent beyond our tender embraces I could stand it no longer. Even though I feared it might stain the memory of my beloved Ambrose I simply could not control the aching that I felt from the lovemaking that had been taken from me. At night I have been sneaking from my private quarters to the nearby hospital tent. I could not see the different men on their cots since the lanterns had all been dampered for the night. I would simply stop wherever my body took me. With a whispered entreaty to the chosen man to not make any sound that could rouse the other soldiers I would remove his trouser. Once his trousers had been laid aside I would lightly stroke and tug him until his staff was long, strong and deliciously irresistible. I had ceased wearing any undergarments many months ago so as to be prepared for any unexpected couplings.

Once I had my secret lover ready I would quickly climb on top of him on his cot. I had to suppress a groan each time I inserted a man's stiff hard staff into my aching moist nether parts. Although none of the men could compare to my beloved Ambrose I felt compelled to continue my nightly forays into the hospital. After I felt whoever I had mounted complete his pleasure inside of me I would rest briefly to control my breathing. Once I had felt my own warmth dissipate I would then quietly slip out of the hospital and back to my own tent.

While on my own cot I have often found my sleep disturbed by thoughts of my naughty secret meetings. The feelings between my thighs felt unsatisfied even after my couplings and I had to press my hand between my legs until I achieved that special feeling flowing throughout my entire being. Oh dear diary I pray that my Ambrose will survive this terrible war and return to me. Until we meet again I will have to satisfy my cravings in any way that is safe.

June 20, 1863

Dear Diary,

There have been rumors afoot that a famous person will soon be visiting the Army of the Potomac where I perform my nursing duties. All the men are speculating that it will be our president himself, he who has led us so handsomely through the terrible trials of the past two plus years. Oh how I wished that it would be. To gaze upon his granite visage would have driven me to paradise itself.

But it was not to be. Instead the president sent his surrogate Vice President Hannibal Hamlin to rouse the troops. And rousing they needed. One short month ago our army once again felt the sting of defeat at the hands of the rebel army. Our army was completely overthrown in the small town of Chancellorsville Virginia. I dare say, and I know that this is scandalous, but I have come to believe that the southern men are simply better soldiers than our own. Our army suffers defeat after defeat at the hands of a ragtag horde that scarcely can be called an army. Our men are in their clean pressed blue uniforms, their shiny buckles above the buttons on the front of their trousers as if they are constantly on parade. From the dead rebels I have seen on the battle field they are barefoot and in rags. Yet they still fight almost to the last man in every engagement. They are rebels, but they are still truly manly and chivalrous men.

The vice president's speech lasted over an hour and the men were soon grumbling. They so wanted to get back to their games of cards and this strange new sport called baseball. I have become somewhat in despair for our union. Our soldiers are playing with their balls when they should be preparing for the next battle.

The vice president spoke of the bravery of our men and how even in the face of defeat they rose up again as the mythical phoenix, growing stronger each time they are cast down, and so forth. He entreated the men to put their faith in the almighty for he would surely lead them to ultimate victory. I trust in the almighty, but I do believe that the vice president would have been better off to tell the men to practice their marksmanship.

After his exhausting speech I headed back towards my tent. Suddenly I heard my name called and the sound of footsteps approaching.. I turned to see who had beckoned me and was shocked to see that it was Mr. Hamlin, the vice president.

Mr. vice president, this is a surprise.

Please call me Hannibal.

It is my great honor to meet the famous Sarah Clarkson, she who had almost single handedly brought release to our wounded soldiers during their time of need.

You do mean relief not release don't you Hannibal.

What, oh yes, yes relief that is what I meant to say Ms. Clarkson. And so Ms. Clarkson, may I join you in your tent so that we can discuss the important work you are doing for our glorious cause.

I decided to be brash and said Hannibal, please call me Sarah. And yes, it would be my pleasure to discuss my interactions so to speak with our brave men.

He gave me a sly grin. Yes, our troops. We surely must discuss them, perhaps after we take care of other matters at hand.

Hannibal was a much older man and rather stout but he had the air of a true gentleman. He held me by the arm as he quickly escorted me to my tent, making sure to open the flap and bow deeply as I entered. Was I imagining it, or did the vice president's gaze linger a little too long upon my back side as I passed him and entered my tent. He made sure the tent was securely fastened and turned to me with that look in his eyes that I had often seen in the men who I ministered to in the field hospitals.

And so my dear Sarah I have been told of the wondrous things you have done with your hands in aid of our wounded troops. Surely you would be willing to show your magic to a vice president such as myself.

I now knew that my actions had reached all the way to the doors of the white house itself.

Why yes Hannibal I would be delighted to demonstrate how I treat our men to a man as important as yourself.

I walked over to the vice president. First I remove your jacket. Then I slide your suspenders off your shoulders so as to give more room as I remove your trousers. Once your shoes and trousers are folded and put aside I help you unbutton your undergarments, if you wear any that is. I myself have long ago given up wearing anything under my petticoats since it is altogether too hot and steamy among the men of our army. And then Mr. vice president I take my soft and supple hands and gently rub the men in their nether regions until, like you are now, their members are turgid and willing. When I see them throb and hear them moan I know that I am doing things properly. Would you like me to show you how it is done Mr. vice president, I mean Hannibal. Would you like to feel the same pleasure that I give our brave wounded men.

He gave a Harrumph as if he were about to begin one of his important speeches.

Yes Sarah, I believe it would be most edifying if I were to see first hand how our men are treated in their time of need.

And so I gave the vice president the same ministrations that I have given our men so many times before. The vice president continued to speak as I expertly applied my hands to his reddening member saying Yes Sarah I do indeed see how the much needed pleasures you provide can bring joy and happiness to our troops after their arduous combat.

In order give him even greater pleasure I unbuttoned my blouse and held my naked breasts against his now bare chest.

Ah my dear Sarah, it as if Aphrodite herself descended from Mount Olympus to engulf me in the passionate embrace of the goddess of love.

I could bear his endless speeches no more and so lifted my breast to his mouth as a mother would do to her crying baby. I must say that I felt a strange tingling throughout my entire person as he suckled. Soon, with a deep sigh as he released my breast from the tight suction of his mouth, the vice president finally understood just how much joy I was truly bringing to our gallant men in the field.

Ah Ms. Clarkson, you are certainly an angel among the hell that is war. Your gentle touch and fulsome breast are surely a gift that the men will never forget.

Would you like me to give you another gift Hannibal. You certainly must be a well traveled man and I but a simple country girl. So I ask you to please enlighten me as to whether I am doing things in the proper manner. I have read that the women of France have a penchant for not merely using their hands but to also bring pleasure to their men with their tongues.. You will tell me if I am as good as the French women, won't you Hannibal.

What, oh yes Sarah please allow me to confirm whether your American style is, so to speak, as well done as that of the ladies from foreign lands.

I could see that the vice president was once more aroused and so as if begging for a treat I went to my knees before him. He was not a large man, but men of importance often rise to their exalted positions in order to compensate for what they are lacking in other areas. As I ministered to the vice president the sound of marching feet could be heard approaching.

Quickly Sarah you must bring me the pleasure you are so practiced at soon. I hear the men approaching.

He was the second most important in the land and so I felt compelled to follow his orders. My ministrations became more rapid. Due to the size I spoke of earlier I found myself able to reach all the way to his abdominal region with my chin soon being tickled by his graying hair. Hannibal groaned deeply and soon the vice president was feeling his pleasure once more. With his chest pounding and his breath shortening he looked down at me as I pulled my head backward, the grip of my lips on him continuing as I did so, and then licked my lips after I had set him free.

Yes my dear, you are surely as good in the use of your tongue as any of the ladies of Europe.

June 28, 1863

Dear Diary,

Something big is afoot. Our army seems to be ready to move but it seems we will be heading north instead of south. I can't believe that we would retreat back to behind our own lines. The men seem so strong and stalwart I have to believe that there must be some other reason.

As the men marched past I couldn't help but feel a rise in my bosom, to see such bravery from throughout our beloved union on display all before me. As they marched past almost the entire army greeted me with a Good morning Miss Clarkson, and Good to see you again Miss Clarkson smiling as they went past. A roar of laughter arose from the entire regiment as one wag with a sharp New England accent said I'd gladly join the invalid corps if it meant getting the special nursing she gives. I did not understand the reason for their merriment but I lightly laughed along with them. This caused an even greater uproar among the men passing by me. It was heartening to see the men marching with sunny dispositions and a strength of purpose.

Along with the preparations of our foot soldiers, the camp has been visited by dashing cavalrymen on their huge horses. I felt an intensity of my lust when I gazed upon these knights of a past chivalrous era. The romance that they bring to our camp is something to stand in awe of. I felt myself dreaming of one of these cavaliers pulling me off my feet onto the back of his steed, taking me away for an afternoon idyll in the forest. Between the heat of the Virginia summer and the heat passing through my body at the sight of these muscular horsemen I felt compelled to get off of my feet and onto a nearby bench for fear that I would swoon.

As the nurse I stayed behind the lines in anticipation of any casualties that may come from our impending battle. I was not able to march as fast as the men and all of the wagons were needed to transport our supplies. It would take me somewhat longer but I hoped to have my hospital tent erected before the battle began. Suddenly I felt myself being swept off my feet as a strong hand pulled me up onto a gray backed steed.

A lovely woman such as yourself should not be marching as if a common soldier. You should not have your beauty besmirched by the dust and mud of the tramping feet of our infantry.

Why sir, you take my breath away. Please hold me in the saddle with your strong hands so I do not fall.

You need not worry about that my lovely. I shall not loosen my grip upon your thin and womanly waist. I am colonel Richard Stoneman of the 20th. Massachusetts regiment. And pray tell, what brings such an impressive beauty such as yourself to the field of battle?

I am Sarah Clarkson. I am in charge of the nursing stations for the Army of the Potomac.

A look of shock came upon the colonel's face when I said this.

Oh lord, so you are the famous Sarah Clarkson. Please forgive me Miss Clarkson, but I first mistook you for one of the camp women who follow our troops in hopes of relieving them of their pay in exchange for their lascivious embraces.

Foolish me. I had never even imagined that such a trade was taking place among our army. I suppose I should have been insulted for being mistaken as a member of that group of women, but strangely I was not. Dear diary, in my mind I felt the equal or perhaps even the better of these loose women in the ways of bringing wanton pleasure to our men in blue.

Oh colonel, surely such a handsome man as yourself would not need to seek the comfort of such women as that.

Perhaps it was the heat of the day, perhaps it was the thoughts of this rugged officer standing before me in a state of undress as he must have done with the camp women in the past but as I spoke to him I placed my hand over the front of his trousers, giving him a gentle squeeze as his horse bucked slightly. The colonel gave me a sly smile.

The battle won't begin for several days and I feel confident that my men will survive without their beloved colonel for a few hours as they march off to war. Come, let us see just how you have brought such storied relief to our wounded, and hale and hearty as well from the reputation that has preceded you, men of our beloved union.

Oh dear diary, I was flush with excitement as my brave colonel galloped off onto a small trail leading into a dense wood. I felt as if I was in a dream. It seems that my colonel had traveled this path in the past for before long the path emptied into a small clearing in the wood. The colonel swung me off his saddle and placed me on the ground with his strong hands. He dismounted his horse and lay his horse blanket on the ground, presumably in anticipation of mounting me.

And so he did. His tall muscular body stood before me in all it's fulsome glory once he had removed his uniform. I still lay on his horse blanket fully dressed. He ordered me to remove my clothing just as if he was commanding his men in battle. I eagerly complied, tossing my dress and undergarments aside in a frenzy. Oh the pleasure I felt once the colonel lay atop me and made me feel that special feeling once more. The sweat arose on both our bodies as he showed me how an officer does his duty. Mere minutes passed before I felt the colonel stiffen and fill me completely. I raised my hips to his thereby bringing him ever deeper. But alas he soon lessened his embrace and then rolled next to me on the horse blanket.

I stroked the colonel's broad and muscular chest as I lay my head on his shoulder. My naked bosoms pressed against his arm as he gently ran his rough fingers along their smooth curves.

Oh colonel that was marvelous. You are such a sturdy and powerful lover.

The truth be told dear diary I was somewhat displeased with his performance, or rather the rapidity of the same. The anticipation of our meeting far exceeded the length of the actual act. His touch, like so many off the other men, was too rough. I have learned though that men are not much better in their moods than the children I once taught in that they feel the need for constant praise.

Thank you my dear Sarah. I enjoyed our mid-afternoon tryst but now must get back to my regiment. I held tightly onto him as he trotted his horse back to the army.

July 1, 1863

Dear Diary,

Instead of moving south to conquer our foes, the army is moving north again. At first I thought that we were once more on the retreat. Word soon spread though that we were marching to Pennsylvania there to meet head on with the attacking armies of the south led by their storied leader Robert E. Lee. Would that we had such leadership in our army!

The battle draws nigh. I can hear the sounds of skirmishers in the distance. Soon the two armies will meet for one titanic death struggle to determine whether those ragged shoeless southerners, so staunchly protecting their homes from our blue clad army, will win their freedom.

The time has come for me to set up my nursing station. I have set up as many cots as I had been able to have brought with the baggage of the army. I also lay blankets as far as the eye could see for those men who overflowed the river of cots outside my nursing tent.

The sounds of battle grow louder. For the first time the thundering of cannon is heard. The mighty struggle for supremacy on the field of battle is to be decided with only Mars, the god of war in pagan mythology, knowing the ultimate decision.

It is almost night before the first of the wounded men is brought to the rear. I lay them on my cots and stroked their rough stern faces with my soft gentle caresses. One of the men opened his eyes, having relived the battle in his mind before I approached. He gazed up at my hands upon his dirty sweaty cheeks.

Oh Miss Clarkson, is that really you? Please Miss Clarkson, I am grievously wounded. Please give me your special ministrations before I pass on to my final reward.

How could I deny such a brave dying soldier? I threw a blanket over him, undid his trousers and before long had him as close to heaven as could be expected in this earthly realm.

Thank you Miss Clarkson. Now I can die with a smile on my face and warmth in my loins and heart.

Night fell. The first day of battle in the small town of Gettysburg Pennsylvania had reached an end with the rebel army in control of the field of battle and on the march.

July 2, 1863

Dear diary,

The wounded men keep pouring in to my station. It is all I can do to bring some small relief to the men, giving them special attention upon their request. But then without warning the unexpected happened. I felt strong hands around my waist soon rising up to my bosom. I closed my eyes and sighed.

Have you missed me my dear Sarah.

I turned around and gasped. Ambrose! How is it possible? Come with me to my tent.

I grabbed his hand and fairly dragged him into my private quarters. I was in such a daze from seeing my Ambrose again that I honestly do not know how I came to be laying naked on my cot, beckoning him to embrace me. I found out afterward that I had nearly ripped Ambrose's trousers from him once we had arrived in my tent I was in such a heated frenzy. He lay on top of me. I gasped. Our bodies writhed together as I begged him to never stop, to stay together with me coupled for all eternity. He let out a series of deep grunts as he pushed and pushed ever deeper into me. I feared that our lovemaking would arouse the suspicion of the men passing outside my tent, but there were no interruptions. Perhaps the sound of our lovemaking was drowned out by the cries of our wounded men.

Ambrose, dear Ambrose, it is such a wonder to see you here. But how is it possible.

I was on provost duty in the earthworks outside of Washington when I heard of this great battle out west in Pennsylvania. I knew that my duty lay with our army in the battle to defeat our foe, not sitting safely playing games of chance all through the day. I climbed the trenches last night and rode steadily to where the sounds of war could be heard. I also knew that you would be here tending to our wounded men. Sarah, I feared that you would have forgotten me.

Ambrose, I believe the intensity of my embraces on your strong sweaty muscular body more than answers any fears you may have had. Come to me once more. I stretched my arms to him and once again felt the lovely pressure of his body as he lay atop me.

An afternoon with my Ambrose was not enough. But he was a man, a soldier, and soldiers must do their duty. As daylight broke over our camp Ambrose gave me one more farewell delight before donning his uniform and riding to the front. Oh my brave Ambrose, I prayed he would be safe from the heat and fire of our foes missiles.

I too had my duty to perform. Day and night without rest I tended to the wounded soldiers bringing them both medical and physical relief. I left many of our men with a smile on their faces despite the pain they felt from the bullets that had torn their bodies.

July 3, 1863

Dear Diary,

The horror of war is all about me. More men than I can handle keep arriving in my nursing station. I have heard from the men that the rebels have put up stiff resistance plunging forward and backward, backward and forward trying to flow through the gaps they find in our lines. My hands grow weak from all the soldiers I have tended to these past few days. But knowing the good job I have been doing, the men continue to urge me on begging me to give them relief.

Despite their strategic superiority and bravery several of the men of the south have been taken prisoner. I am intrigued. I have heard and read of these men but had never actually seen them. They may be our foes but they are not our eternal enemies. Even these southern men need to be nursed from their wounds. I went to the holding area where these captured rebels were being kept. The guard allowed me to pass once I explained that I needed to determine the needs of our prisoners.

Gentlemen, I am Sarah Clarkson, a nurse here to tend to your wounds.

Well that's mighty nice of you Miss Clarkson. We are but prisoners however, and with the blessings of the almighty we have remained unscathed from the fury of the battlefield.

Such strange accents! I have never heard such a thing save perhaps what I imagine that the English knights of old must have sounded as they guarded their kings and queens in their castles. And the men themselves have such a lean and tough look about them.

Sir, I said to their senior officer. Please tell me if you would, why exactly do you fight so fiercely against us.

What I heard next was something I never expected. The southerners have been portrayed in the press as nothing more than filthy traitors. Instead with a strong stentorian voice the leader of these men gave his explanation.

The northerners have tried to suppress our economies to the benefit of their own cities. The restrictive tariffs that have been put on the exports of our goods has caused an economic depression which has fairly ruined our economies. The tax base of the country was designed to bring growth to the manufacturing sector of which the south has little but the north has a surfeit. We could not long survive under such a system. It has brought ruin to many of our small farms and left their people in despair.

But what of the slaves, don't you fight to keep them in bondage.

Do you dare insult me Miss Clarkson. To Hades with those damned slaves. We would just as soon be rid of them as not. If the northern politicians hadn't kept us under such severe restraints then there would be no need for such human bondage. I say that if the northern abolitionists love the slaves so much then we would gladly trade them for the idle men of your New York, and Boston and Philadelphia, who bought their ways out of conscription and who do nothing productive to fill their days. Let these idle white man take the place of the black man on our farms and we would gladly be rid of the institution of slavery forever.

I was taken aback. I had often followed the simplest answers in life despite being a trained teacher. The majority is the one who controls the flow of information. Far from being ignorant traitors it seems that these men had an honest and true complaint against our government. To see such men of conviction, fighting for a cause that has been distorted by my own leaders, sent a feeling of near outrage through my veins. Here thousands of men have been killed when simply adjusting the tax code could have prevented all this terrible carnage.

Sir you give me much to think on. Perhaps we can discuss it further in a more secluded area.

I gave him a small grin whose implication could not be misconstrued.

Miss Clarkson, where I go my men go.

Why of course sir, that is indeed noble of you to have such strong feelings for the needs of your men. There is a stand of shade trees a little further east. Perhaps we can retire there to discuss the politics of the day, captain?

At your pleasure Miss Clarkson. Please, do lead the way.

Off to the woods. The long beards and filthy hands of these rebels sent shivers down my spine as I felt them touch me all about. It was a different kind of pleasure than I had experienced before. To sneak away with these men who had rebelled against all that I held dear and to give myself to them so wantonly made me nearly faint with excitement. How many men had their way with me. I could not count.

Our secret meeting only came to an end when a scouting party from our master at arms went in search of the missing rebels. I stayed behind, hiding behind a tall tree, as the rebel captain explained to their captor that he and his men were merely trying to get some relief from the heat. The entire rebel mass broke out in a fit of laughter at the captain's words.

Never mind that you damned rebels. Get back to where I can see you.

I must say dear diary that these shoeless dirty men gave me more pleasure than any of the clean well uniformed men of our northern army ever had.

My brief meeting with this group of bad rebellious men makes me long for more.

July 4, 1863

Dear Diary,

The day of American Independence seems especially joyous this year. The terrible warfare that has raged for the past three days has resulted in thousands and thousands of casualties both blue and gray. It has also resulted in the rebel army returning to Virginia. Our army is so exhausted from the fury of the past three days that they are unable to give chase.

The hospital tents are overflowing with the victims of the battle. Even so more men are left outside in the elements still lying of the field of battle, unable to return to the camp. The commanding general has ordered me to help find and then give assistance to these men, the ones that could not return under their own power. I am to put small flags next to the living so as to identify them and have them brought to our hospital.

What I saw was shocking to my core. A vast tract of land covered with the dead and dying. I steeled myself for my duty and determined to follow the groans off the living in order to identify them for removal. I have been given orders to only identify our own living and not those of our foes, but I find this to be unnecessarily cruel. A man is a man, regardless of the color of his uniform.

The heat of the summer day combined with the cries of the wounded almost overcame me. Nevertheless I did my duty. As I worked my way through the late field of battle I discovered a strange phenomenon. Almost to a man the wounded called out for their mothers, not their wives or sweethearts, to come to them in their time of need. Giving relief as only a mother can, I undid my blouse and to each man crying for his mother I rocked him in my arms gave him my breast to suckle telling each of them You have been a good boy and mother is very proud of you. Come suck of mother's teat my brave young son and let a restful sleep come upon you.

I must have given such relief to the agonizing pain of hundreds of men that day, making my breasts tender come nightfall. The soreness and swelling of my breasts was of small consequence compared to the bullet and cannonball injuries of the wounded.

I returned to my tent ready to fall into the deepest sleep of my existence to that point. As I prepared to undress and lay myself down there was a voice outside calling my name. I had taken to sleeping completely without any clothing due to the heat of the Virginia summer so I had to quickly cover myself. I took my blanket and wrapped it around my naked body.

Please come in I told the late night visitor. It was my great surprise to see the commanding general of our brigade.

General, you have caught me unprepared for a visit. Would you like to sit with me on my cot? The general flushed, turning red in his face and clearing his throat.

Ms. Clarkson – please call me Sarah general – Very Well, Sarah, I have heard of your great works you did today in aid of our brave men. Very few, man or woman, north or south, would have had the strength to carry out such a grim but necessary task. You are truly deserving of the title The Divine Being of the Battlefield. I shall be recommending you to President Lincoln in hopes that congress may recognize the great service you have given our country in it's time of great peril.

I was ecstatic almost beyond words. Without thinking I leapt from my cot to give the general a hug. I did not realize that my blanket had slipped off as I did so, leaving me holding myself in all my nakedness against the general's rough woolen uniform.

Thank you general, thank you. I am greatly honored to think that our president would even become aware of such an insignificant woman as myself.

I realized that as I hugged the general that he had something not insignificant beneath his trousers.

Would you not like to stay with me general? I do so get lonely at night.

Sarah, after your long day servicing our men are you not too fatigued to spend time with me.

General my breasts are tender but my loins ache even more so. Come general, show me how your strong body can overcome me just as in your strength of mind you overcome our foes. The general lay next to me, only to rise as the dawn broke and leave me.

Oh my dear diary, I tell you in secret that I am dreadfully lonely. I am surrounded by rough strong men, but I have nobody to confide in but you. I long for another woman to befriend and to share my life and my thoughts with. This war has become so bloody that the need for more nurses grows by the day. I shall ask for permission to recruit a corps of my own, a corps of female nurses to aid me in my nightmarish work. Perhaps then I will also find the female companionship I crave.

July 6, 1863

Dear Diary,

I had the most strange encounter today. It was something that I had read about only one time in one of the books I secretly read about, this one about some roguish pirates from a century ago. To think that would become involved in such an adventure was most incredible to me.

The battle had been so devilish that the dead and wounded seemed to fairly flow in from the battlefield to our hospital for the past four days. I did my best to provide as much relief as I could to the wounded men, in the way that I knew how to do best. The men all seemed to be satisfied with my private ministrations. Everything changed when I came upon one soldier who appeared with a wound in the left shoulder.

The soldier did seem to be in some small degree of pain. I checked to make sure the wounded shoulder was properly bandaged. Then, as I had done so many untold number of times before, I unbuttoned the soldier's trousers to give him additional comfort. When I reached into the soldier's trousers I found nothing. I reached all around before speaking.

Oh poor soldier, you are grievously wounded! Your manhood seems to have been shot away. Poor poor soldier your life will be forever transformed as a result.

Quiet you fool, do you want to expose me? I am no man. I am a woman who has chosen to live as a man so as to defend our country. Come, let me show you. She took my hand and put it between her slightly spread legs. I gasped in surprise.

Soldier, you surely seem to be prepared just as the other soldiers always are, but in your own way.

You silly girl, just how little do you understand the ways of the world. Give me your hand.

Oh dear, you are so moist.

Put your finger there, that's it, now put it in deep and move it all about.

I felt my body flush – here I was bringing pleasure to a woman dressed as a soldier just as if she was one of the men. I stood there in shock as she placed her hand on top of mine and bucked her hips against it. Without warning she grabbed my head pulling it down to hers. I could not speak. Her lips rubbed against mine and my mouth was forced open by her tongue. Her whole body stiffened as she moaned deeply into my mouth. She relaxed but I was still in shock.

You are a good girl. What is your name?

Sarah.

Well Sarah, I am Roberta. But you must call me by my soldier's name of Robert. I feel that you can give me much comfort until I am released to service. Where is your tent?

I pointed.

Do you sleep alone?

I nodded yes.

May I visit you tonight in your tent?

Yes I said in a soft yet deep voice.

Silly girl, do not be so surprised. It is my belief that a person, man or woman, must try and find what pleasure they can in this cruel and harsh world. Do you not agree?

Yes.

Then I tell you that I find pleasure with a woman in my bed. Does that shock you?

Well, I must say, it does, but I must also say that I find an unexpected excitement simply envisioning it. I will tell you a secret: My mind has frequently wandered to the idea of what it would feel like to have another woman in my cot with me. Men can be so rough and think of nothing of their own pleasure. The gentle touch of a woman is what I believe would be a welcome diversion.

Hah, then let us see what we can do to bring excitement to each other on your cot. I will be by after nightfall this evening. I will show you pleasure more than any man could. Now, go about your business and we shall meet later.

Oh dear diary, I was confounded by the meeting I had just had with Roberta. Up to that moment what she was describing was beyond anything I had ever imagined. Yet still, I had that special feeling between my legs in an intensity I had not felt in a very long time. The rest of the day was spent in an otherworldly state of mind as I found myself in an ever growing anticipation of Robert's promised nighttime visit.

July 7, 1863

Dear diary,

How can I begin to describe the events of the night before this. At nightfall I repaired to my tent eagerly awaiting the visit of my strange new soldier friend.

By this date I had been with many men and felt I knew what to expect each time I mounted one. I could not fathom how two women could possibly bring such pleasure to each other as a man and a woman could together.

There was a whisper at my tent flap.

Sarah.

Yes, please enter.

I could see Robert enter by the light of the candle in my tent.

Let us dim that candle. I do not wish to have our encounter this evening to become known to others. There, now it is dark and we can act in private. Remove your clothing completely and then lay back on your cot.

You do so come across as a man, don't you, with your tone of command Robert.

Hah, I tell you Sarah that not every woman feels that she fits in the role of the soft and weaker of the two sexes. I had always preferred to play at the game boys played in my youth. I announced to my mother and father one day when I was five or six years old that I did not wish to wear dresses but preferred to be in the trousers and rough shirts that the boys wore. At first my parents just laughed at me and called me a silly little girl, but I persisted. I refused to leave the house if I was forced to wear a frilly dress and after a time my mother and father allowed me to impose my will upon them. I felt happy beyond description the first time I went to play with the other boys in my trousers and shirt. They did not notice as long as I played well. I imagine that the others in our small village must have whispered behind my back, but my father was a prominent man in the town so nobody dared to comment aloud. I have lived my life ever since as a man. When this war broke out it was natural to me to follow my country into battle.

Robert, that is an amazing story. I must admit it is not something I had ever heard of outside of a story book of pirates of days past.

I felt Robert's uniform against my naked chest as she lay next to me on my cot. She wrapped her arms around my body and pulled me tightly against her. Once again our lips met, her rough kisses combined with her tight grasp on my naked breast. Her hand was replaced by her mouth as she broke our kiss and began to suck my nipples into her mouth. As she sucked her hand went between my thighs and forced my legs farther apart. Just as I had done to her earlier, now so I was exposed to the pleasure of her manual ministrations.

The feeling was amazing to me, the combination of all the nights I had spent with my own hands between my thighs at once.

Quiet you fool, control your moans, you will get us caught.

I could not stifle my sounds with any degree of success since the feelings were so intense. I felt Robert's hand over my mouth as my body shook. More kisses upon my lips, bodies rolling over so that Robert lay beneath me, hands on my shoulders pushing my body downward.

Kiss me between my legs. I will instruct you on how to do so.

Diary, I must say I was in a haze and a fog all at once as I allowed myself to be pushed between Robert's legs.

Robert instructed me in the ways to please a woman even if she was a woman masquerading as a man. She grabbed my pigtails and directed me where to go, where to put my tongue, how deep to go, how fast to move my tongue, the proper way to use my fingers. Her many instructions were hard to follow but I must have been a good student.

More so than any of the students I had taught in my past as a school teacher, I was quick to learn my lesson. As Robert grunted her pleasure I was shocked to suddenly feel a liquid fill the soft area where I had just been using my tongue, a liquid unlike any I had ever seen or tasted before. Robert held my head tight and harshly instructed me to clean it all up. I had no choice but to comply.

Once I had finished lapping Robert clean she pulled me up for another kiss. She held me tightly in her arms but I remained silent of any complaint.

I have been with many women, and even a few men who were comfortable with my secret, but you are surely the most talented of them all Sarah. Will you allow me to continue to visit with you?

Yes Robert most certainly, please visit me nightly if you wish.

Hah, you truly are a good girl Sarah. I will be over to visit tomorrow after sundown.

Oh dear diary, I do not know what to make of these feelings I have. Our love that night had been so intense that I craved for more, but the idea that this was such a forbidden type of love made it all the more exciting. Being so roughly and powerfully handled by Robert gave me a special thrill as well. I count the minutes until tomorrow's sundown when I shall see her again.

August 1, 1863

Dear diary,

Is it possible for one woman to love another? It seems impossible, perhaps something out of ancient Greece where the gods would perform a Bacchanalia for the people where all manner of licentiousness would take place, or perhaps the rare woman sailing with the pirates of old in men garb. But in this modern age in this Christian country it seems all but impossible.

Yet here I am, feelings of love that I never imagined were possible for my seductress, my Roberta, or as she prefers, Robert. After our first night together Robert would sneak into my tent every night We did not have much time together so I would wait for her naked under my bed sheet. It takes so long to remove a woman's clothing with all the corsets and petticoats and buttons and ribbons that I would waste precious time with my lover Robert.

When she arrives in her soldier's uniform it takes but a minute to remover her trousers and tunic, slipping under my sheet as soon as she too was unclothed. We would embrace and kiss in the special way that she had taught me. Not just a small peck on the lips. She taught me that the kiss can be a way to arouse your lover. She had me open my lips so we could softly rub them together. The first time she put her tongue in my mouth and rubbed it against my tongue I pulled away. But she pulled my head back to hers and soon our tongues rubbed against each other, tip to tip, entwined, rubbing up and down. It gave me such a warm and tingling feeling throughout my body that I was amazed that this could happen from merely kissing another.

Robert would have me suck on her nipples while she moans and whispers hoarsely to suck harder and harder. She takes my hand and places it on her warm, damp sex urging me to rub it all up and down as she bucked against my hand. Sometimes my finger would accidentally slip past her outer area and enter into her bringing her to paroxysms of joy. After rubbing my hands between her legs long enough feel her begin to tense up she would then pull me off her nipple to her mouth, giving a deep hard kiss as her body shook. Once she descended from her personal heaven we would hug our naked bodies against each other, bosom to bosom.

Diary, I am almost too afraid to tell you what happened next. Soon merely having me rub her with my hand was not sufficient to satisfy my insatiable Robert. One night when I was preparing to do my regular ministrations she spread her legs wide and began to push me down between her legs. I have a surprise for you Sarah. Feel what I have between my legs.

Oh dear, how is this possible. It is as if you have grown a man's member. I have heard that some women still practice black magic but I never thought that I would encounter it in person in such an unusual way.

Oh you dear silly nave girl you make me laugh so. There is no black magic, merely an artistic representation of a man's member carved from whale bone and polished to make it possible for smooth entry into a woman. I have heard the men talking of your special treatments and my inquiries have led me to the conclusion that you have been with many men. I know that you have the knowledge of how to properly use a man's member. I wish you to do it to me. One end of the polished whale bone goes into me to hold it in place. The other end is for your use. Now please Sarah, treat me as you would the other soldiers It will bring me great pleasure.

The world is a strange place I have discovered dear diary. To think that if I had stayed as a school teacher in New Jersey I would never have experienced the ways of men, and of a woman who in all manners desires to be a man. I love my strong and powerful Robert yet I can't help but pity her. To go through life having to keep so deep a secret every day must be very trying on her mind. I wanted to make her happy, to help her feel as if she was accepted in the world by at least one person. I did as she said.

The bed cover was pulled back and I treated Roberta's whale bone member as if it were that of a man. Roberta's eyes were on me as I used my mouth on the smooth decorative device between her legs. It was carved in the exact shape of a true male member. I had taken many a man between my lips so I treated Roberta to the show that she so desired.

Sarah you make me feel so excited watching you treat me so. I feel that my deepest dream has finally come true. But enough of the magic of your lips. I wish to penetrate you as a man would. On your hands and knees. I shall take you from behind so I can further watch as your body shakes from my thrusts into you.

But Robert, I have never done this in such a manner. Of course I had done so with my dear Ambrose but I wished to fulfill Robert's fantasy as much as possible. I have only climbed on top of the men as they lay in their sick beds. I do not know what to do.

I will show you Sarah. Now do as I said, get on your hands and knees right now.

It felt as if she had transformed herself into a true man the way with her husky growl as she ordered me to offer myself to her in a truly exposed way. I felt a strange thrill as Roberta climbed behind me on my cot.

Spread your legs wider Sarah. That's it. Now don't be surprised as I enter you, it may feel different than you have felt with the other men.

Oh Roberta, it feels so wonderful. You are more thrilling to me than any other man I have been with. Come and bring it deeper into me. Grab my hips harder and make love to me like the man you are.

No more Roberta. From this point onward you shall call me Robert. I no longer wish for you to see me as a woman.

Yes Robert, I will. You will be my man and I will be your woman.

That's a good girl Sarah. I have dreamed to have a woman as my wife since as far back as my memory goes. I feel my arousal reaching it's peak Sarah. Push yourself back against me and I will hold you tight. Yes Sarah, yes you bring me such pleasure. Oh Sarah, Sarah I can hold back no longer.

Yes Robert I feel your body tense. Allow your feeling to freely overcome you. Your breathing is so short Robert. I feel so happy as you lay against my back and hold me tight by my breasts.

Robert rolled off me after some minutes pulling me into a tight embrace as we shared a long passionate kiss.

I am so happy Robert to have such a big strong man sharing my bed, making love to me as a real man does. I desire to make love to you nightly. Stay here with me each night. I long for a man's embrace each night as I lay alone in my tent.

I will be your man each night but must leave by dawn's breaking. I am supposed to be an invalid and should I be seen to recover I will be sent back to the troops of the line.

Do not speak so Robert. I dream that we will be together forever. Now please hold me in your strong man's embrace so I can fall asleep with a smile on my face.

September 3, 1863

Dear Diary,

The battle in Pennsylvania has devastated our army. Although our forces had much greater numbers than our southern foes we are unable to continue on the attack due to our tremendous losses. The best we could do is rest on the field and lick our wounds, preparing to fight again next year since this year's fighting season is past. It is to be presumed that the Confederate army is doing the same. The one bright spot is that we have received news of a victory of our forces in the west at a riverfront village named Vicksburg. Name after name of towns and villages whose names will forever be remembered for the bravery and horror that took place in and around them.

I still live in fear, but not of the southern armies over the border. I live in fear that I will lose my dear Robert. We have had to live a secret life, where we have to hide what Robert has under her uniform, where I worry that Robert will be sent back to the battle front, where I dread that we will be caught in our nightly embraces.

Robert's wounds have largely healed and I say this from close personal inspection every evening. Since the fighting on our northern front has ceased after the great battle Robert has been kept behind in our encampment on provost guard duty. The army lives in a fear of it's own, fear that the southerners will attack again at any moment.

Yet I must say dear diary that as stressful as it may be, the secret life I have been leading gives me an indescribable thrill. Knowing that I can be caught with Robert and our affair exposed at any moment makes my heart beat faster. It is the story as old as time I suppose. Like Eve with the apple in the Garden of Eden, that which is forbidden is that which is most desired. The thrill and excitement of knowing that what I am doing is wrong is overwhelming my sense of right and wrong. I feel as if I have become a very bad and naughty girl fearing yet at the same time strangely attracted to the idea of being punished for my secret misdeeds.

September 10, 1863

Dear Diary,

My love for Roberta, Robert, is deep. She visits me each night under cover of darkness to find me lying naked on my cot waiting for her strong embrace. To see her removing her soldier's uniform in the pale moonlight always makes my breathing become heavier. I believe that she has taken to wearing her member beneath her uniform at all times now since every night as she removes her trousers it can be seen jutting straight and stiff from between her legs.

It took awhile for me to get used to receiving it since it does not have the combination soft yet hard feeling that I had become used to when mounting the invalid troops in our hospital. That it remains ready for constant use is a true pleasure though, making for extended lovemaking that can last the entire night if we wish.

Robert's rough behavior gives her an air of manliness greater than most of the rest of the men in the army. At first I believed it to be an act – she must act more like a man than the rest of the men so that she does not be discovered as a woman. However she does not have to hide her secret from me, therefore it is my belief that she has completely given in to her desire to be a man. My acceptance of her as she wishes to be has likely broken through the final mental barrier stopping her from fully seeing herself as a man.

I love how he holds me tightly. I love how he forces his tongue past my lips as we kiss. I love how his kisses press hard against mine. I love the feel of his hands on my bosom. I love the feel of his lips on my nipples. I love how he strokes me between my legs. I love the feeling as he enters me with his long staff. I love how he talks to me as we make love, telling me what a dirty girl I am and how I am even more wanton than the camp girls who set up tent outside off our encampment. These words have an effect on me that I cannot explain in words. All I can say is that it makes me buck against Robert harder, drawing him deeper into me, when he speaks to me so. We roll and thrust over and over until I feel a wonderful warmth build up throughout my entire being. I nearly faint, almost as if it was a pleasant entrance into heaven, when the feeling suddenly bursts forth all at once. Robert commands me to control my cries of joy, but I am beyond control. She stifles my moans and cries by pressing her lips to mine as I caress her tongue with mine.

When I finally descend from the celestial realm I have the earthly pleasure of seeing my Robert looking down at me with lust as I smile up to him. We collapse into each others arms and fall into a sweet sleep, awaiting the rising of the sun which signals the sad farewell I must give to Robert each day. Sometimes I am extra naughty and rouse Robert out of his sleep, urging him to make love to me once again before he must leave.

October 29, 1863

Dear Diary,

I have been sly. I could bear to be away from Robert during the daytime no longer so in my naughtiness I have created a ruse to allow us to be together.

I am the senior nurse in the army now, so my duties during the lull in the fighting are largely to oversee the actions of the other nurses under my command. This being so, I was able to convince my supervising doctor that Robert needed special care caused by battle fatigue and announced to him that I would give Robert the special care that he needed. I am not positive but it appeared that the doctor gave me an inquisitive look as I made this pronouncement. Nevertheless any misgivings or queries he may have had were not ones that caused him much concern since with a shrug he agreed to my idea.

And so my idyll began. Robert moved into my tent. We lay together throughout the day every day keeping each other warm with our bodies entwined. Even in Virginia the weather turns cold in the end of the year, so our natural heat helped stave off the cold air outside of our cot.

I have taken to nursing Robert in a special way. Although it is not common practice to bathe regularly among the men, especially not in the colder weather, I have decided that Robert needs to be washed each day. To anyone who asks I reply that though they may be brave soldiers they are not nurses so they should not presume to question my nursing skills. That always guarantees and end to the questioning and an apology.

It is a true joy to be able to see Robert in the daylight. I bring in a warm basin of water and then peel his uniform off. With a soft cloth that I have dipped into the warm water I wash his body from head to toe. He moans with pleasure as I rub him up and down and into every one of his bodily crevices. I dry him off with a towel I have heated next to our stove. He takes me and kisses me deeply before helping me remove my own clothes. We fall together onto my cot and give in to our passion. Oh my dear diary this is the happiest period of my life. I pray each night that it will never end.

December 25, 1863

Dear Diary,

Robert's battle fatigue continues. I must help her overcome her affliction daily, treating her with love, care, and passionate caresses. I fall asleep with a smile each night as Robert holds me tight in his strong arms. I have seen two and one half years of brutal bloody conflict which is enough to make any person, man or woman, have dreadful dreams. Yet with Robert holding me all my fears and concerns slip away.

We have set up a life together as man and wife. I have begun to dream of a life together outside the army as well. Lying in bed one night I told her that perhaps we should simply leave. I am not bound in any involuntary way to this army. I have chosen to be here and can choose to leave at any time. Robert entered the army under false pretenses being a woman pretending to be a man. Although she lives as a man fully now, that does not take away from the fact of her false enlistment.

Yet Robert to his credit pushed aside such dreams. He said that a true man lives with honor and that it would be dishonorable to simply leave the army before the war had reached its conclusion.

A tear fell from my eye as Robert held me tight. How long with this terrible war last? When will I be able to live the life I want with the man that I have fallen in love with? I decide to simply surrender to my happiness and not give a care to the possibility of a sad future.

January 31, 1864

Dear Diary,

We have been discovered! It appears that one of the men had been wandering around the camp and had heard the muffled sounds of joy emanating from my tent. Being naturally curious he spied upon Robert and I as we held each other upon reaching our mutual ecstasy. He himself was so aroused by the vision he beheld that he lost his footing and fell through my tent flap. Robert and I both let out small shrieks of surprise at this unexpected development.

The soldier leered at Robert and I and then looked confused. What sort of madness is this. Are you two women? I see a soldier's uniform but no soldier has a woman's bosom. Explain yourselves.

I am a soldier and a woman at once. Do not be shocked.

But what is that between your legs. Are you some monstrosity that has both male and female traits?

How damnably stupid are you soldier. It is merely an aid to better make love to my woman.

I am thoroughly confounded, I cannot speak.

That is well, do not speak of this or you may find yourself on the wrong end of a musket.

I had to intervene. I had seen so much death that I could not stand anymore.

Soldier, do not be frightened by my companion. Come here and I will relieve any of your concerns. Take off your trousers and come lay with me. My legs are held wide and I await your entry.

He was stunned, but not too much to climb on top of me once his trousers were dropped. He thrust hard and fast and I urged him to give me more of his manhood in a way that would arouse any man. If I were to be believed then he was the greatest lover since the ancient Greek god Adonis himself. I do not believe it necessary to say, but my words had him finding his pleasure in but a short period. He lay heavily atop me once he had finished.

Robert, green with jealousy and purple with anger all at once, grabbed the soldier by the scruff of his neck.

Get up you and leave at once. She is mine and you shall have no more.

Show me how it is done.

What in Hades do you mean.

I mean show me how it is done, how two women can make love using your artificial member. Show this to me and I will speak of none of this to a single soul.

Robert looked outraged and went for his knife. I grabbed his arm.

No Robert, no blood is to be shed tonight. Perhaps it shall give us a new type of thrill to be watched as we bring each other joy.

Not a word said Robert drawing his finger across his neck in a cutting motion as she glared at the soldier.

You frighten me. I understand that I must not speak of this if I wish to live.

Good man, now watch and see a show that you will remember for the rest of your days.

Oh dear diary, what a show we gave him. I licked and kissed Robert's whale bone member. Robert went between my legs and give me a complete licking all around. I suckled her and she me. We kissed long and deep. Robert ordered me onto my hands and knees and took me from behind, holding my hips tight as he thrust into me in a near frenzy. It seemed that being watched truly did excite Robert. Robert reached under me and fondled my breasts as he continued his thrusting. I squealed my womanly delight. Robert grunted and growled like a man. Too soon Robert and I both collapsed. The intruder stared at us with his mouth agape.

You have had your show. Now leave and do not return.

The man awakened from his amazement at that and quickly fled my tent. I rolled onto my back, beckoning Robert with open arms and legs spread apart.

You enjoyed being watched as we made love unless I miss my guess Robert.

Hah, is it that noticeable. You are right my dirty little girl, I found myself overcome with lust knowing that we were being watched in our most intimate moments. Did you not feel the same way?

How could I not, what with being treated with such ferocious thrusting and fondling of my breasts. I found myself swept up in your frenzy. But upon reflection it is more than that. The idea of getting caught in our illicit affair has always given me a feeling of excitement in my loins. Now that it has happened it was as if my secret naughty dream had finally come true. I did indeed enjoy having his eyes upon my naked body as you had your way with me.

You make me laugh Sarah with your secret dreams. Perhaps there will be a way in the future after this war ends that we can engage in such exhibitions together. I am aroused once more merely thinking of it. Open your legs wide for me Sarah. I must have you again.

MARCH 6, 1864

Dear Diary,

I know I have been derelict in writing yet it is only so because of how happy I have been. I have spent he past month in blessed domesticity with my sweet soldier Robert. The fact that this blissful period might ever come to an end is one that was never entertained by either of us.

Sadly life does not stand still, not for me and not for anyone in the history of man. A fear has crept into me and I believe Robert although he is too strong to admit his feelings. The weather warms and to the army this means that the battlefields will erupt once more. More death, more pain, more lost limbs and shattered bodies. The worst I have seen over the past few months were the occasional mild frost bite.

This war has been so interminably long that the men have developed ways over the years to preserve their health despite the poor sanitation and exposure to the various vagaries of the weather. The winters are surprisingly cold in northern Virginia, just as the summers are unbearably hot.

The president it seems has become frustrated at the inability of our generals to create a stratagem that could bring about a final resolution to this bitter conflict. To date the leaders of the army have either been timid in the face of the determined foe or in the alternative have not been able to create a plan of action that outwits our greatest adversary, the renowned general Robert E. Lee who guides the main army of the South.

Despite his retreat from Pennsylvania in the year past, our army has had little success in conquering the territory under his military jurisdiction. We have but a foothold in the environs surrounding our capital at Washington city.

In what is perhaps an act of desperation the president has appointed a new general to lead our army. He has appointed a new commanding general, General Grant, whose sole recommendation for command of the army is his lack of strategic ability but his willingness to sacrifice more and more troops to merely overwhelm his opponents. This was the strategy he used out west to wrest control of the Mississippi river from the Confederates. It seems that the president has decided this brutish man is what is needed to club the enemy army into submission.

In anticipation of such a strategy all but the most seriously wounded soldiers still in our hospital have been ordered back to the line. Robert has been deemed fit enough to return to combat. He is to deploy tomorrow. My heart is full of anguish and trepidation as well as a feeling of pride at his soon to be brave and valorous actions in defense of our country. As much as I admire the constancy and resolve of our foes, it has become apparent to me that our president is correct in his determination to hold our country together as one.

MARCH 8, 1864

Dear Diary,

Robert has left the hospital and been sent to join his former unit near the old battlefields of the previous three years. Our final night together is one which I will have in my dreams for the rest of my days. The knowledge that we would soon be parted made a greater sense of urgency to our lovemaking. As soon as the rest of the army had retired to their cots and fallen asleep Robert and I felt that it was safe to have the most vigorous time we have had to that point. Our arms entwined to hold each others naked bodies against each others. Our lips met in a long almost desperate kiss, neither of us wishing to let our tongues, our mouths, part. Our hot bodies rubbed against each other. Robert's lips upon my breasts caused me to gasp. I held her head against my bosom as she continued to suckle me, causing my nipples to shrivel and harden. The moisture between my legs was greater than it had ever been. It positively flowed in anticipation of what pleasure I knew Robert would bring. I was surprised that Robert did not immediately enter me as I had expected but instead slid down my body and pushed my legs apart. His tongue on my wet soft spot drove me to the heights of ecstasy to the point where I feared my howls and groans of delight would alert the sentries and have them investigate the source of these strange yet exciting noises. In time I felt the warmth build up throughout my body as it had so many times in the past. My body stiffened and Robert held his tongue on that special spot that seems to be the source of so much of my wildly tingling delight.

Robert did not hesitate. Once my mind had left body Robert immediately pulled himself hovered over me by holding himself with his strong arms. He immediately plunged into me, meeting no resistance whatsoever due to the stream between my legs. I bucked my hips hard and fast against Robert to bring him as deeply as he could go into me. I squealed. He fairly snorted. It was as if two wild animals were engaged in a match to the end, one crying out in high pitched squeals as she was dominated by the humping beast who had grabbed hold of her.

I reached the gates of heaven once more seemingly at the same moment as Robert. He pushed as deeply into me as he could possibly do all the while grunting rhythmically in time to my own cries of delight. Our bodies relaxed and slowed as Robert fell on top of me. Neither of us could speak. We merely held our naked sweaty bodies in a tight embrace, our breasts pressed against each others. We fell asleep exhausted in our lover's embrace.

I awoke the next morning to find Robert gone. He had left to join his company which was already moving it's encampment to be nearer to the upcoming field of carnage soon to come. I could not leave my cot that entire day. I was visited throughout the day by the other nurses under my command but no amount of nursing could repair the hole ripped in my heart.

April 29, 1864

Dear Diary,

There is an electric air about the camp as the armies continue to prepare for battle. Our hospital has been moved closer to the army's encampment in expectation of another harvest of death. I spend each day walking among the assembled troops in hopes of spying either of my dashing brave heroes, Robert or Ambrose. Sadly I have not been able to catch of glimpse of either of my beloved men.

It is a wonder that any person, man or woman, can survive such pain which reaches down to their very soul. I have not just one but two men for whom my heart aches. How will I survive? Is my pain any less than the bullet wounds which scar the men who flood into our hospital each spring and summer? I walk about as if in a daze. I must force myself to beat back this deepening dark despair. I have my duty to do for our army once the year's battle season commences.

APRIL 30, 1864

Due to the terrible carnage this war has wrought ever more nurses have joined my corps. To my surprise one of the nurses approached me and said I know you are heartbroken Ms. Clarkson, but perhaps I can help you heal. My name is Lucrecia. We in your corps were aware of your relationship with Roberta, Robert, but we held our tongues. You see, we are all independent spirits. One must be so to break the bonds of a life preordained for a woman. Women of such a like mind must stay together, and keep our secrets together.

I had an idea of what she meant but I had to find out completely. What is your name again?

Lucretia.

So Lucretia, shall you come to my tent to elucidate me about what these secrets you speak o may be?

A sly smile passed over Lucretia's lips. Of course Miss Clarkson. It shall be my pleasure. And perhaps yours as well. I frowned slightly at that comment.

Soon we were in my tent with the flap tightly closed. Speak to me Lucretia.

As you know our sleeping quarters are far separated from the men's. This gives the women freedom to express themselves in a way that would otherwise be forbidden. In a word, we share our beds each night. We often fear that the sounds coming from our tents will alert the guards. She gave a light lilting laugh as she said this.

So Lucretia, you think that by being my bed mate you can help relieve the anguish I feel over Robert's departure?

Given the opportunity I believe that I will be able to bring you a modicum of relief, perhaps more than that. I may be able to make you forget your woes completely.

Show me.

Lucretia approached me, unbuttoning her blouse as she did so. Once it was unbuttoned she removed it completely. Her breasts were of moderate size and clearly had never seen the sunlight. Small pink nipples tipped her breasts. She bent down and kissed me softly as I sat on the edge of my cot. Would you kiss my nipples Miss Clarkson, taking her right breast in her hand and offering it to me. Call me Sarah I said just before wrapping my lips around her breast.

Oh Sarah we are certainly of a kind she said as I took as much of her breast into my mouth as I could. Her breast in my mouth, I sucked while at the same time caressing her nipple with my tongue. She breathed deeply and sighed as I sucked her. Oh Sarah I am overcome. I cannot control myself. Please reach under my dress and touch me in my woman's spot. I shall surely reach my ultimate arousal should you do so.

I did as she requested. My fingers met her wetness. I slid them along her until one of my fingers found its way past her outer barrier. I continued to suck her breast while my finger went into her. Suddenly she stiffened. Her whole body shook. She tried to stifle her cries of delight so that we would not be uncovered. Soon she relaxed and looked down at me in a daze.

Oh Sarah, you amaze me. I have not felt such a thing in all my years. I beg of you, let me become your new lover now that Robert has been sent to the front.

I brought you pleasure then? I said coyly, in false words for I already knew the answer.

You are indeed a little scamp Sarah. Could you not tell how I enjoyed the sucking of my breast and the stroking of my womanhood? You tease me.

I smiled at her in a humorous way. Of course I tease you Lucretia. The quivering and quaking you displayed gave you away.

Sarah, may I stay with you or at least visit with you in your tent? Please?

I thought on this for a moment. Yes you may Lucretia. Perhaps you will indeed be the antidote for the loss I feel for Robert. But for now go. You may return after nightfall tonight if you wish. I wish to see the nightly exploits of the other nurses of which you spoke. Afterwards we can retire to my tent for the night.

Yes, thank you Sarah. Would that I could command the sun to fall behind the horizon at this very moment so that I would be able to wrap your soft woman's body in my arms and hold you against me all the sooner sooner.

You wish to command the sun. Your eagerness makes me long for our meeting as well. Come, kiss me before you depart. We kissed deep and long, in anticipation of our nighttime meeting.

MAY 1, 1864

Dear diary,

The events of last night make it near impossible to write, both from sheer physical exhaustion but also from the excitement of the night time revels.

As sun set Lucretia came to my tent. I asked her in and as soon as the tent flap closed she pulled me into her arms, placing her lips on mine in a near frenzied kiss. She ran her hands over my entire body over my dress. I considered just bedding her right then, but remembered my desire to meet the other women in the nurses quarters. Lucretia, your lips and hands make me steamy. We can carry on our passionate embrace later though. You promised to introduce me to the other nurses. She pouted. Can they not wait for another night? I find myself near unable to control my passion for you. Your lips on my breast, your exploring fingers, that is all I have been able to think of all day long.

I smiled. Soon Lucretia, soon, we can continue. But first I expect you to keep your promise to me.

Reluctantly Lucretia took me to the large log cabin that was the nurses quarters. Upon entering I was treated to the aroma I had been presented with during my most intense meetings with both Ambrose and Robert. More so with Robert. The scent of a woman's passion was different in a sweeter way than that of a man. Men smelled stronger and often made me turn up my nose. The smell in this cabin was more of a musky perfume. I looked about and saw that all of the women were naked, or at least nearly so. I was surprised yet aroused at the same time. The women were either coupled in sensual embrace or tittering at some private joke. I was amazed that such a thing could be taking place in the environs of a massive army during time of a bitter deadly war.

Ladies, this is our leader, the great and renowned Sarah Clarkson.

Surely Lucretia, you must not speak of me so. It is if you found my name in a work of history and brought me back to life. With this the ladies all gave a variety of laughter, both large and small. I found myself surrounded by a mass of naked women, their soft hands caressing me, their soft lips kissing me. I could hardly breath. The feelings rushing through me were so intense I felt nearly faint.

Come join us Sarah. The world beyond this cabin's door is filled with terror and woe. In here you will find a peacefulness and loving care that you will not find anywhere else. Please remove your dress. You will see how freeing it can be in both body and soul to join your sisters without the raiment that confine us so. These heavy garments were created by men to oppress us. They desire our sex yet at the same time fear our bodies. They have created these garments to accentuate our sexuality while at the same time totally covering our flesh. It is an absurd situation that could only have been created by the male sex as a means of forced self control of their sexual desires. Don't you agree Sarah? Don't you find the layers of clothing that women must wear to be rather ridiculous Sarah? They force us to wear such unweildly clothing as a means to control us.

No stranger to the exposure of my flesh to others during moments of love, I was not averse to being without my dress while in the bed. However being exposed to a large group of women was another thing. After some hesitation I overcame my discomfort and undressed. Oh diary, the lady's were so right. I felt as if I had never been so free in my life. The admiring words and glances of the other nurses made me feel all the more at ease.

I spent an hour or more carousing with and listening to the bawdy jokes of the other women. I laughed and laughed. After some time I felt someone behind me. She began to gently squeeze my naked breasts with both her hands. Come Sarah, I cannot wait a moment longer. Let us repair to your tent so as to engage in our private explorations of our bodies. A smile passed my lips at the thought of my soon to be private and intimate rendevous with my new bed mate. Lucretia and I bid our adieus to the other ladies. Most did not notice as they were otherwise engaged with each other in the cabin's cots.

June 1, 1864

Dear Diary,

This past month has been a whirlwind! The men are attended to in my usual way, giving them relief from their wounds, both physical and mental relief as I am wont to do. As is to be expected in this endless conflict the soldiers spend their days in this hellish place, burning in the hot Virginia sun. In the not too distant past I would have helped them out of their heavy woolen uniforms to give them the relief they earned as brave soldiers. Now these days the best I am willing to offer them is cool water from a well that has been dug next to my cabin.

Why is this so you may ask. It is because of my new passion for my lover Lucretia. She and I have become inseparable. I feel that if I were to continue to give the men any release then it would be a form of cheating on Lucretia.

And in the end all that I desire is my Lucretia. Although we may go about performing nursing duties during the daylight, at nigh we are alone in our passion. Lucretia ugoes to the ladies portion of the nearby river to bathe some time before I finish my daily rounds. Once I am done I retire to my tent. It is there that I am daily presented with the sight of my Lucretia, Lying naked on my bed per body propped up on her left elbow as her long languid body stretches the length of my cot. She has acquired in some unexplained manner a supply of cosmetics and perfumes brought here all the way from Paris France. With this she paints her lips a bright red and sprays herself with the sweetest perfume. This vision brings my breath short each time I am presented with it. Some would think that repetition would bring too much of a familiarity but for me this is not so.

Each night when I return I fairly tear off my clothes so I can fall into the hot embrace of my perfumed lover.

Lucretia and I have spent the past two fortnights laying with each other. Our tongues rub against each others as our lips gently press. The stroking and kissing of each others breasts brings from each of us moans of delight. But this is merely a prelude. With our exploring hands we find each others wetness. Lucretia lays on her back and gives a sultry smile, gently pushing me by the shoulders at her juncture. That which our tongues have done I now do by myself as Lucretia moves her hips upward to greet me. I delight in the way she bucks and twists as I use my experience in female anatomy to find just the right spot to bring her joy. She often whispers for me to use my finger upon her as well as my tongue. I know I have done well when I feel her entire body tense and shiver. She holds m y head tightly until her body finally relaxes. I love the dazed look she gives me, her mouth slightly open in surprise as she lets loose her grip and I look up at her. She grabs me and pulls me up to her, giving me an even more deep and passionate kissing than even before.

Lucretia often reciprocates, but I do not require it. I get my pleasure from simply seeing the smile on her face, the feel of her breasts in my hand and the shuddering passion that I am able to bring her.

June 8, 1864

Oh dear diary, I feel that I am in love! I go about my days in an etherial haze. All that I can think of is my nighttime affairs with my lovely Lucretia. I have begun to make errors in my work for I cannot concentrate. Too frequently these days I hear the men cry in pain as I probe inside their manhood to administer the tincture of mercury which is used to cure the pox brought upon them by the camp women. It is quite funny but the camp women have been given the sobriquiet of "Hookers" surely named after our General Hooker who was known to frequent the camp ladies and who allowed them free access to the men in their tents.

Lucretia and I try our best to keep our relationship from being known, but it is difficult . We gaze into each other's eyes and repair to a quiet glade in the woods as ofteen as we can to bring our lovemaking out of the night and into the light of day, albeit filtered by the leaves of the shady tree under which we lay. We carry a camp blanket with us each day, ostensibly to use for any man who may have the chills from a fever, but in truth for Lucretia and I to lay on the ground in more comfort. The cool breeze on our naked flesh drives me mad with desire. Oh diary it is the most amazing feeling, to be with my love while at the same time feeling a certain amount of danger should we be caught.

I fear that our near constant love making is taking its toll on Lucretia. She has started to fatigue easily and goes into her slumber as soon as she pulls me up to kiss her. With a wan smile she gently holds my head against her breast and strokes my hair. Soon after she falls into a blissful sleep****

I must ademit dear diary that I am conflicted. I like the feel 9of a man, the strong grip holding my body, the fullness they can pro9vide, Yet aside from my Ambrose or perhaps even Robert I have had no great feelings for any man. It was merely a physical union with all of the men I have been with theses past three years. And I see now that I have never felt any true and real love for any man, I have felt no honest actual emotion or passion. Yet with Lucretia I feel a deep unexplainable joy. Her touch, her feel, her softness, they give me a feeling far beyond anything a man can provide. Men and women are so different. If I could switch between either as the mood came upon me I believe I would have a fulfilled life. I am not a complete fool dear diary. I know that should I be married or engaged to a man he would have me arrested and flogged should he find that I desired to be with a woman. In the alternative I should find myself blackmailed again as with the soldier who uncovered my secret life with Robert. Perhaps in the end I am meant too be alone, just as I was when I was a teacher in New Jersey. I do not know when this war will end but the constraints of our society will likely cause me to return to my dreadful life that I had before the war. How can I ever be content merely reading of romance now that I have experienced so much as I have during the past few years. I feel happy to be with Lucretia, but I feel bereft that once the war is over my life of passion and adventure will forever be taken away from me.

June 10, 1864

Oh my oh my dear dear diary, the most horrible news! My sweet lover Lucretia has come down with a sudden cough. I am deeply worried. I have seen many soldiers die from uncontrollable coughing, perhaps even more than from the wounds of battle. The doctors are totally at a loss of even how to treat such a terrible disease. They refer to it as consumption but know nothing more than that.

JUNE 13, 1864

Dear diary,

I am filled with unhappiness once more. My sweet friend, my lovely Lucretia, has died from consumption. In three days she went from one small cough to being choked to death by a relentless loss of breath. She did, in effect, cough herself to death. The doctor's could do nothing. They told the undertaking corps to prepare a grave for her. I knew this but I would not tell Lucretia. As her nurse and her love I could do nothing but try and give her as much comfort as possible during the terrible three days of her ever increasing illness. I held her in my arms through every day. The doctors told me to quarantine her since my exposure to her cough could bring the same malady upon myself. I did not care. I would not abandon my Lucretia in her most dark days. She died in my arms this morning. I am not even overcome as I would be expected to be. Instead I feel my mind turning numb. The horror of this war, the horror of this life, how can one stand it? Yet still I must do my duty.

Lucretia's body was taken away and buried far from the camp. The doctors feared her disease would spread to the men, further depleting their ranks before the upcoming battle season. This fear must have overtaken the entire camp for other than myself and the black men who shoveled the dirt over her bare flesh there was no others to mark her passing. Not even her friends, the other nurses, showed. She died in my arms and she was laid to rest with only me to see her off. Farewell sweet Lucretia. If there is an afterlife I hope that you will find the freedom and release you so desperately longed for on this earthly realm.

June 15, 1864

Dear Diary,

How terrible these past two months have been. The new commanding general Ulysses Grant has lived up to his fierce yet blundering reputation. It seems as if there is endless fighting with ever vaster numbers of wounded men being sent to our hospital.

The battles began at the beginning of May with general Grant blindly sending our army into the tangled wilderness of Virginia. Our troops found themselves trying to fight their way through a dense dark forest for no apparent reason. The general could easily have ordered the army to bypass the wilderness and engage the enemy without marching into a ghostly morass. Instead he seemingly was attempting to achieve a somewhat shorter path than he would have had by simply marching them over open ground. The result was our troops being devastated by armies of snipers hiding behind every rock and tree in the wilderness. The general was finally forced to retreat from this terrible death filled forest. All night the cries of the men left to die a hellish death by fire in the forest set aflame by the sulfurous powder of our muskets were heard.

Despite the shocking number of casualties from that one battle general Grant continued his deadly pursuit of his nemesis, the renowned general Lee. At a small village named Cold Harbor the pursuit ended. General Lee was determined to make a stand once more against our army.

Using a strategy that best suited the much smaller army that he had at his command, general Lee had had his men dig a series of deep intertwining trenches to both guard against the approaches of Richmond and to stop general Grant's massive onslaught.

And so despite his huge army and his attempts to simply crush the army of general Lee, another failure was wrought. In the course of one short morning general Grant ordered four successive attacks against these trench works. The final result was over eight thousand of our soldiers killed or desperately wounded with but a fraction of this number of casualties on the southern army's side. At last the soldiers of our army refused to charge any more and so once again general Grant was forced to retreat.

I find it almost impossible to believe that the country will allow such terrible bloodletting to go on almost endlessly. I believe that the president has made a terrible blunder in appointing this madman as our army's commander.

I am fairly overcome by the number of wounded I must tend to. There are acres of men who must each receive the whatever medical care we can give them. It plays upon the mind to be surrounded by such gore all day for weeks at a time. The sole consolation I have is that I have come across neither Robert nor Ambrose among the wounded, nor are either of them on the lists of the dead posted outside the headquarters encampment. I still hold out hope that I will feel the gentle loving embrace of my Robert with her sad and dangerous secret or the rough overwhelming yet dashing manliness sweeping me away of my Ambrose. It is these thoughts that keep me awake at night, pressing my legs together in the hopes of bringing forth a smattering of the pleasure that my men have brought me in the past as each of them floats through my dreams.

July 20, 1864

Dear Diary,

We have been playing what can best be described as a game of a big cat chasing a small mouse throughout the summer, only this mouse is a deadly one. After the horror of the first two months of this season general Grant determined that he could not withstand yet another large battle against his clearly more competent opponent. He has been in consultation with the president throughout the summer it has been said, and appearances are that the determination to fight a war of small battles, slowly picking away at the enemy, has been decided upon. This has led to the slow yet noticeable reduction in the ability to continue the fight by the southern army. While this was going on throughout the summer our hospital stayed behind near the battlefields of the spring.

Our hospital was kept busy enough with the results of those two failed battles as to not be able to accommodate any further wounded, yet they continue to be shipped from afar to be cared for by our doctors and the nurses under my charge.

With such a huge influx of men needing tending I found it almost impossible to bring them my special relief all but single handedly. I resolved to bring a number of my nurses into my secret way of caring for the men so that this special treatment could reach the greatest number of wounded as could be done. At first I chose the nurses who seemed to have the greatest spirit and the most brazen and open behavior. Those with the largest bosoms seemed to be the most open with the men and so I chose a group of them to let them know of my special work. Some of them flushed with embarrassment yet most appeared intrigued. I explained in both words and demonstration how to best bring the wounded relief while at the same time remaining discrete. This training often brought paroxysms of laughter as one or another of the nurses made a bawdy joke regarding the size and shape of the men they had known in the past. And so began the increase in the special treatment of our wounded soldiers.

July 31, 1864

Dear Diary,

Yet another mad blunder by our commanding general. After chasing general Lee's army for a month they were finally forced into trenches in the countryside surrounding Richmond. General Lee excels at building such fortifications so by skillful use of his engineering acumen he has thwarted general Grant's attempts to capture the Confederate capital. In frustration general Grant dug a massive tunnel under the Confederate trench works and attempted to blow a large enough gap in their lines so that our army could march through and into Richmond.

Instead a large crater was caused by the underground explosion into which our army was promptly sent. Instead of marching through a gap in the Confederate lines our army was sent to march into a hole which can only be described as large enough to hold an entire army. Our poor poor soldiers were slaughtered almost like never before as Confederate cannon rained canister and shell upon the hapless soldiers standing helpless in the hole.

Having achieved nothing except additional slaughter, general Grant has decided to besiege the southern army, hoping to starve them into surrender. Those who were not slaughtered in Grant's crater were taken prisoner by general Lee's army. I only say this since despite such a massive blow against our army, very little wounded were sent back to our hospital.

I once again find myself searching the list of the dead for either of my brave and handsome suitors. Neither of them ever appears on any list. I pray this means that they are unharmed and will one day return to me. But where oh where can they be? I miss them both so, dreaming each night of the heated lovemaking they have both given me. It almost seems that my time with each of them was but a pleasant yet salacious dream. I miss the feel of their hands on my breasts., their breath on my neck, their tongues entwined with mine.

July 31, 1864

Dear diary,

A rather odd series of events have begun to interrupt my life. The camps religious leader, a parson Crumb, has a wife Agatha. This wife Agatha Crumb seems to have through various intrigues and outright spying determined both the nature of my ministrations to the wounded soldiers as well as the different lovers I have taken over the past few years. She has told the parson of this and expected him to report me to the commanding general so that I could be punished. Her husband it seems told her to give Christian compassion to the wayward sinner who is known as Sarah Clarkson. Others have thanked me for the good works and relief to the soldiers that I bring. It turns out that I am seen as nothing more than a sinner by the parson and his wife. Despite being told by her husband to be a Christian Mrs. Agatha Crumb decided to ignore the words of her husband. The nosiness of this woman could lead to my discharge from the nursing corps and returned to the dreaded life of a school teacher to the ignorant little children at the behest of their equally ignorant parents.

August 12, 1864

Dear Diary,

It seems my troubles just increase. The parsons wife has actually begun to follow me around the camp calling me in loud voices a heathen sinner who must be cleansed form the army. She has been trying to get an audience with the commanding general. She has apparently has been petitioning to have me arrested and sent either to long term imprisonment or alternatively the gallows! In the name of Christian morality! I am under near constant surveillance. I have seen her hiding behind trees taking notes of my every move.

Word around the camp is that it would be more useful to her should she follow her own husband about the camp, especially after each nightly meal. He is seen daily choosing after each evening's repast the fairest and youngest of the soldiers to give special ministrations to, so to speak.

I apologize dear diary, I should not be so mean. If a man should decide to be with a man it is not my place to judge. If I do then I become no different than the terrible monster known as Agatha Crumb. I can certainly understand why the parson would choose the company of young men over the company of his angry harpy. And again who am I to judge when my own proclivities seem to be towards members of my own type, strong and bold women.

August 14, 1864

Dear Diary,

My life has become near unbearable! After the parson's last weekly service the insufferable Agatha leaped up and pushed her husband aside. She then spent ten minutes ranting about me, my evil sinfulness and how any person who consorted with me was condemned to eternal damnation and other such nonsensical words. I fled in both shame and fear but heard the words of the men shouting her off the stage as I ran to my cabin.

What can I do dear diary? Should I leave the army and return to my old employment as a school teacher? I dread such a fate, but if my continued presence would b e detrimental to the good order of the army then perhaps I should go. I feel trapped and simply because I have brought my own form of relief and happiness to the poor wounded soldiers and misunderstood denizens of our glorious if not so victorious, army.

AUGUST 19, 1864

Dear diary,

Just as I was about to pack my things and leave the army the unpleasantness brought upon me by the immoral Agatha Crumb has fortuitously become no longer a concern. After attempting to get our general to take action against me for my perceived sins to no avail, she threatened to contact the president himself. The general demanded that the parson gain control over his wife. Being a rather meek and quiet man with his own secrets the parson made no effort to do so. The men could be heard grumbling at her interference as well. Her endless and loud railings against me had brought about the unintended effect of that which she sought.

Last night a single rifle shot could be heard. This was a common event in the army so no alert was called. This morning the body of Agatha Crumb was found spread on the dirt in the center of the camp. Her body was stiff and cold. She had been dead for several hours. There were no witnesses to the event so no charges could be brought. Her death was listed as an accidental gunshot during times of war. She was buried that same day, her husband saying the prayer over his body, no-one but a soft and handsome young private brought there to console the parson attending. It is said that the two off them took a long walk in the woods surrounding the grave site, arm in arm.

There is a general sense of ease that has taken over the camp. The parson himself seemed strangely dispassionate knowing that his wife was shot and buried. He seemed almost relieved at this turn of events. I hope you don't find me spiteful dear diary if I do not refer to it as an unfortunate turn of events.

AUGUST 29, 1864

Dear Diary,

Things have been slow since the last great eruption of violence at the end of July. We have laid siege to General Lee's army around the environs of Richmond so tedium abounds. An interesting yet strange and sad development has arisen however. With the encircling of the confederate army large numbers of slaves have fled their captivity and found their way to the army. They are referred to as "Contraband" as if they were some form of ill gotten property. And under the law I suppose they are; they are not citizens yet they are no longer in the possession of their former owners.

I have to admit that I am intrigued by these people. They seem completely odd and different from any person I have ever seen. Their skin color truly is black, the texture of their hair is unlike the white man's hair even at it's it's waviest. And their facial features seem so much fuller and handsome than the people of my own race. I must admit to some degree of jealousy of their women. Even under their thick woolen dresses it is clear that they have a far more womanly shape than your average white woman.

I let my imagine run wild the other day laying in bed wondering of how fascinating it would be to have one of these black women come to my tent and undress, allowing me to explore her naked body, rubbing my hands all along the rounded curves of her smooth brown breasts and hips, feeling her full soft lips against my embarrassingly small and thin ones. That special feeling rose in my loins at the thought. Perhaps some day I would have that pleasure. Until then all I could do was live in my dreams.

September 4, 1864

Dear Diary,

The freed slaves have set up their own little village just outside the perimeter of our camp. I have made the strange acquaintance of one of them. He has been made into the camp cook due to his previous employ as a cook for the slaves on his former plantation. As such he has the experience to create basic but nourishing loads of food for large numbers of men. Previously he had been feeding the hundreds of slaves on his former abode. Now he is using his skills for the large numbers of soldiers in our camp.

I was curious as to how he was made into a cook. He was such a large, strapping and muscular man that I felt sure that his strength would have been put to greater use in the cotton fields. The word that has spread in the camp is that he is so deficient in his brain that he could not properly pick even the least number of plants without destroying them.

One day shortly after he was brought to our camp he arrived at my tent carrying a bucket of a savory smelling stew.

How is you misses. I done brought you some special vittles just for your dinner. I makes it special myself. Hopes you likes it misses.

It does smell delicious. Please tell me, what is your name.

I'se be called Columbus misses.

Listening to this man's speech almost drove me mad.

Columbus, you are a free man and I was a school teacher prior to joining this dreadful war. It would bring me great pleasure to teach you as if you were one of my former students. If you are to truly survive in this hostile world you must be able to speak properly. Once we accomplish that we can move onto other skills. Would you like that Columbus?

He gave me a quizzical look, as if he kept a secret that he was unsure that he wished to share. Finally he spoke.

Miss Clarkson, you are too kind. I assure you that my manner of speech is merely a ruse to, as you say, survive in this world.

I was shocked. But Columbus, how is this possible. The reputation that you have is one of a simpleton. He gave a short and bitter laugh.

Sadly a person of my race must live in the shadows for fear of his life. The white race must treat us as their inferiors and keep us in chains in order to keep their economic dominance. If the black man is free and equal to the white man then it could cause a disruption in the economy. It is better for them to keep us in ignorance and chains than to run the risk of a black man taking a job from a white man.

I was shocked, stunned, speechless.

But, but, Columbus, how on Earth did you learn to speak so well. Surely your former master must have prevented you from getting an education. And I am sure that you would have been severely punished if you had been caught learning.

T'is true Miss Clarkson, that should I have been caught in the act of learning I would have faced the lash. But I am discrete.

But Columbus, you did not answer. How did you learn to speak so well.

Miss Clarkson – please call me Sarah – Very well, Sarah, mine is a tale both uplifting and sad. I was made to do the heavy work around the manor, lifting logs, shoeing horses, and any other brainless work that required nothing more than brute strength. As such I spent most days in the environs of yet outside of the manor itself. One day I noticed the little mistress of the house, Annie, sitting in the shade of a tree with something in her hands. I politely and deferentially asked her what brought her out in the hot sun. She told me she was reading a book. Then she asked if I would like to listen to her read. I knew it was forbidden, especially since she was a child of but eight years old, however somehow her simple question made me feel at ease and so I took her up on her offer.

Well Sarah after that day little Annie and I would meet under the same tree most days. At first she would read her simple child's books to me. Then one day she asked if I would like her to teach me my letters so I could read to her some days. It was forbidden, strongly forbidden, for a slave to learn to read. But how could I turn down such an opportunity. Well then for some splendid weeks afterward Annie and I would study together and before long I was able to read. It was a revelation to me. I knew then the power of the written word to change the world. But as most often happens in life this idyll came to an abrupt end. One day Annie and I were seen sitting together under that tree and Annie was forbidden to ever speak with me again. The sadness on her face was most heart breaking. Her final Goodbye Columbus to me practically had both of us in tears.

Some few days later, just as dusk was setting, I heard a small yet urgent knock on the door of my slave cabin. When I opened the door I found a volume of the Complete Works of William Shakespeare on my doorstep. Little Annie, my true friend little Annie, I saw running in the distance back to the manor house. It was the dearest gift that any person could ever have given me. She was a wonderful person. Even at the young age of eight years old she had more humanity than any dozens of grown men and women put together.

Oh diary, I was in tears after Columbus's tale. She truly was a great person Columbus.

Indeed, Sarah, indeed. With this book in hand I studied in secret. With much effort I was able to work my way through the entire massive book. With repeat readings I have become literate. My absurd slave speech is my cover which allows me to interact with the white man's world in a relatively safe manner. Once I am truly free I will give up the charade.

Columbus, you fill me with amazement. The lie has been exposed – the black man is equally as smart as the white, perhaps even more so to be able to prevail under such dreadful oppression. I truly admire you.

Sweet Sarah, it is you who are the amazing one among us for you have no qualms at speaking to a black man as simply a man and not be swayed by the color of my skin at the outset.

A noise outside my tent caused Columbus to start.

Yea noise, then I'll be brief. It has been an honor to speak with such a great woman as yourself.

Columbus I must see you again.

Very well Sarah, we shall indeed continue to meet though it must be as some form of subterfuge. We shall find a way, as people of intellect are able to do. For now I must away, but we shall meet again another day.

An officer on his horse was outside my tent turning in his saddle as if searching for something. Columbus stepped outside. Yet as he left my tent Columbus made an amazing transformation once more, reverting back to his slave speak that he had used as a protective cover all these years.

Columbus, where have you been. You are missing from the cooking area.

Oh I'se be sorry Cap'n suh, but I'se jus been making sho miss Sarah gets her vittles. She don't eats wif de men and I don't wants a lady to miss Columbus special stew. I'se goin' now Cap'n. I'se makin my special possum stew tonight jus like the mend likes it.

What, possum stew, no Columbus, no, go to the commissary and draw the rations of beef assigned to each company.

Tha's a mighty fine idea Cap'n. Ain't no mo possums round here noways. I done ketch 'em all, and all dem squirrels, rabbits, muskrats and polecats. They ain't no mo left of any ob dem no how, no suh. I done cooked 'em all up fo the men.

What? How can you make possum stew if there are no more possums to catch? And did you say polecats? Do you mean skunks? Have you been feeding the men skunks?

Yassuh Cap'n, Columbus makes a fine polecat soup. The mens they lubs it da best. Dey says it reminds dem of they girls back home. Mm, mm dey eats dat polecat stew likes it Chrismas dinner.

The Captain made a shocked and disgusted face, perhaps wondering if he had been fed Columbus's skunk soup.

What, are you mad, how can you feed the men skunk? We have an entire commissary filled to overflowing with fresh beef. Oh, I am sorry Columbus. I have forgotten my manners. I sometimes lose sight of the fact that the people of your race are but children. Now there there, don't be upset. Be a good lad and get the beef for the mens dinner.

Yassuh Cap'n suh, I'se gwine gets da beef fo the soldiers. But if I sees a polecat I sho'ly will ketch it and gives that extra flavor to da stew tonite. The men's sho'ly do lub dey polecat stew. Mm mm.

The captain turned his head in revulsion and just at that moment Columbus turned back to me and gave me a knowing grin and a wink.

SEPTEMBER 19, 1864

Dear Diary,

After our first meeting Columbus and I have become fast friends, though we must keep our friendship hidden. As before, the thought of being caught in an illicit liaison gives me an indescribable thrill.

My entire time in the army has been one of thrilling adventure. I have lived more in these past four years with the army than my entire thirty years prior. My friendship with Columbus is perhaps the most forbidden of all. Ambrose and Robert were my secret lovers and my adventures treating the men in my special way, and even my tryst with the confederate captives, were not as seriously forbidden as my befriending a black man. It is a cruel world we live in where merely associating with a person who is treated as an inferior because of the color of his skin can cause a terrible and perhaps deadly alarm.

When we can find a free moment to sneak away Columbus and I spend our time discussing literature, Shakespeare in particular, philosophy, the arts, the natural world, political concepts and all other manner of discussion. I have found an intellectual equal in Columbus. I honestly say to you dear diary that I long for the secret meetings I share with Columbus.

October 30, 1864

Dear Diary,

So much has happened since I last wrote. I believe that I have broken a great taboo and consequently I feel a constant thrill in my body all hours of the day.

Columbus and I continued to meet in secret as often as we could. This war of attrition, the siege of the Confederate army around Richmond, has left little for me to do since there is a paucity of casualties to care for. Those whom I have tended to after battle are then removed to either full army hospitals up north or, if possible, sent home to recover with their loved ones. A lot of my work now deals with treating the various personal diseases the men contract from the female camp followers. There is a standing order forbidding the men from these liaisons but no order or law will prevent men from getting their pleasure wherever and whenever they can.

Columbus and I had been having our own liaisons but only for the pursuit of an intelligent and intellectual comradeship. Our friendship grew and one night as I lay in my cot thinking of the time I had spent with Columbus that day I had a sudden flash in my mind of how it might be to make love to him. I was shocked at the thought. He was such a strong and muscular man that I was intimidated by him. And of course his being a black man it was unthinkable that he and I should couple – if caught it could be a death sentence for him. But once the genie has been let out of the bottle as in the stories of the Arabian Nights there is no putting him back. I lay awake for the rest of the night my breath short and heavy my thighs pressed together as I imagined how it would feel to have his huge arms holding my slight body.

November 10, 1864

Dear Diary,

It has happened, and it must forever be kept a secret. I have opened Pandora's box and all the lust and deceit in the world has escaped.

As many a day before Columbus and I were meeting in our hidden spot in the woods discussing all that we have discussed in the past. The sun beat bright and warm despite the lateness of the season. This is called an "Indian Summer" though I know not why. I decided to be brave.

Columbus, have you heard the men or their officers speak of my nursing ministrations for the wounded soldiers, and how I have taught the women under me to provide the same type of special nursing. I blushed as I asked this.

Your reputation is much spoken of throughout the camp, especially about how only the women with the largest bosoms are used as your assistants. I must confess that though I find it hard to ken, the idea of such a thing intrigues me. It is certainly a novel way to bring relief to the grievously wounded if it were indeed not the lies of the devil. In this world women are seen as either the wholesome and saintly mother keeping the family together and the hearth warm or alternatively as women off ill repute. Those women who are not married and who leave their father's home are almost certainly described as harlots, nay to be blunt – as prostitutes, no matter what their true vocation may be.

I found the overwhelming lust flow through my body as he spoke.

Would it shock you Columbus if I were to say that all of the mens talk is true and likely not as fully known as what I have indeed been engaged in. Would it shock you if I were to tell you that I have engaged in far more liaisons of various physical manners than the most slatternly off any of the camp women?

Columbus looked at me neither in shock nor puzzlement but with comprehension. He smiled softly.

Sarah, it has become my belief that all men and women should be free to live their lives as they find best for themselves no matter what their situation. Having been in forced bondage for all of my years the greatest dream I ever had was to simply be able to do as I wished while doing no harm. From all indications you have done good work and brought great happiness to a vast array of men who otherwise would have succumbed to their distress. It is clear that the things you do give you a form of relief as well. Simply because the majority rule and morality frowns upon such a thing does not make it wrong in the eyes of the almighty. You have done far more good than any possible harm both for the men and yourself.

You talk of your closed and frustrating life in a small village in New Jersey, a life of unhappiness and almost despair. That was your own slavery, being forced to live a life that you were not meant for. You are free now Sarah with me and do not have to keep your actions in the darkness. You are an angel to the men, the Divine Being of the Battlefield as I have heard the men say.

Hearing Columbus give me the approval and freedom from shame that I had feared would never come made me feel a great affection for him. I suddenly found myself flinging my arms around his thick muscular shoulders.

Oh thank you, thank you Columbus. You do not know the distress I have felt these past four years fearing at any second that I would be uncovered and imprisoned. You have given me peace in my mind that I so desperately needed.

I could feel Columbus's body tense.

Sarah my dear friend despite our beliefs it would cause great consternation should you be found to have your arms around me. To hug or in any way become intimate with a black man would certainly mark you with the letter of shame on your dress.

I do not care Columbus. Let them bring me before their court martial in their hatred. I will feel no shame.

I pulled out of my hug but kept my arms on Columbus's shoulders. We looked into each others' eyes, a smoldering heat rising from both our bodies. Our faces slowly drew towards each other. Our lips lightly met. This was more than I could control. I pressed my lips to his more fervently, opened my mouth to his and had him do the same, finally engaging hm a kiss like that should be done between lovers. Columbus wrapped his strong arms around my slender waist as I wrapped my arms around his neck. Our kiss lasted forever it seemed since I never wanted it to stop.

I pressed my body against his. Remove your shirt Columbus and I will do the same. I have an uncontrollable desire to press my naked flesh to yours.

In a flash like a bolt of lightning we both were unclothed from neck to waist. I gasped as I saw Columbus' chest. He was filled with strength, his strong thick chest glistening in the heat of this unusually warm autumn day.

I rubbed my hands across his chest in amazement at how manly he appeared. I groaned as he held my breasts in his large yet soft hands. I nearly fainted as he brought his lips to my nipples and gently sucked them one by one into his mouth, caressing them with his tender lips.

Oh Columbus, I am overcome. I feel I must faint. No, do not stop, keep sucking my breasts. It brings me a full measure of delight when you do so.

As Columbus made love to my breasts I found myself almost in a hypnotic state. Without being aware what I was doing I found my hand slowly working its way to his trousers.

What I felt broke me from my dreaminess. I pulled back in shock.

Columbus are you hiding some form of weapon in your trousers? Do you mean to cause me harm after the friendship we have developed? He looked confused.

Whatever do you mean Sarah. I certainly do not wish you any harm.

Then what have you hidden in your trousers.

Why nothing. I shall remove them to ease your concerns.

Columbus stood. I fell backward of the log upon which we had been sitting.

Oh dear, oh dear, Columbus is this really true or is it some form of alchemy. I have never seen such a thing in my life and I have seen plenty. Is it possible that this massive club protruding from your nether region is truly your male member?

Yes Sarah, it is all which the almighty has blessed me with.

Oh Columbus, I am beyond surprised. All of the myriad of men I have been with are but slender pencils. You have a flagpole planted in your loins.

I fear that I shall not survive should we couple. I do not know what I shall do.

As a man of science investigating a newly discovered species so to I approached Columbus with a curious eye. I tried to wrap my hand around his member but found myself unable to. I attempted to put my mouth around the tip of him but could do no more than stroke him with my tongue.

Columbus, I so do desire to bring our bodies together yet I fear I will not be able to. I am but a slender little girl and you are a massive redwood tree. I shall have to consider if this shall be possible.

As you wish Sarah. I have had this said about me many a time in the past. The girls on the plantation would always titter and giggle when I walked by. Only the women with the widest hips would approach me. Although they always told of the great pleasure I brought them I could not help but notice the hitch in their step once our love making was through.

Voices were heard in the tree line. Columbus we must go our separate ways. We shall meet again tomorrow. Tonight I will ponder how or even if we shall be able to become lovers. We fled in different directions though I wondered how Columbus could even walk let alone run with such an encumbrance.

December 1, 1864

Dear Diary,

We are in winter quarters once again. Although the news is always favorable to our cause, we still have not been able to reduce our foe. They fight as stoutly and resolutely as they always have, now suffering the pangs of hunger and exposure caused by our blockade. General Grant, like so many others before him, was unable to beat the great General Lee in open combat. The only way he has been able to prevail is by cruelly starving the southerners to near death.

But enough of war. Let us speak of love. Columbus has found a way for us to be together daily. While cooking the dinner for the troops one day shortly after our amazing meeting in the woods, Columbus spilled a trough of boiling stew onto his left hand. The burns were shocking to behold, nearly down to the bone. He was sent to me to recover and I applied a full dressing to his hand.. perhaps exaggerating the extent of his injury. Why would I do such a thing you ask dear diary. It is because of a plan Columbus revealed to me. He had purposely burned himself so that he would no longer have to work feeding the men. Instead he said that I should apply to have him become my assistant in my nursing duties.

It was a wonderful plan, reinforcing in me the belief in Columbus's great intellect. And so I followed through on his plan. I assured the captain of the commissary that Columbus would never be able to work in the kitchen in the future. He agreed to release Columbus from his duties and sent his regards to Columbus saying that he was the best cook the army had despite his lack of intelligence or training. I was disgusted at this expression of pure ignorance.

I next was allowed a meeting with the commanding general in our company and was granted permission to keep Columbus as my aide. Our plan complete, Columbus constructed an extra room to my winter cabin in which he was to stay. I do not need to tell you dear diary that this addition was rarely used. Although I had a wood burning Franklin stove in my cabin it was the warmth of Columbus's bare body against mine that kept the winters cold at bay.

January 3, 1865

Dear Diary,

The cold winter has been kept away by the love between Columbus and I. It took many a try but with great effort I was finally able to feel Columbus's huge stiff tree trunk in my body.

The first time he entered me completely I let out an involuntary cry of pain. I begged him to stop to remove himself from me but he would not. He held me tightly until the pain subsided. Slowly, gently he moved himself inside of me a little at at time. It hurt for sure but with repeated gentle swaying I began to feel the pleasure that only a man can bring a woman. My body began to move in rhythm to his. I felt myself sliding up and down as my great pleasure began to grow. It finally overcame me as I felt Columbus fill me at the same time.

I gasped loudly in uncontrolled glee for a great length of time until I could take no more. I felt as if my heart would burst from the contractions of my body from Columbus's great member entering into me. He lay atop me for a length of time finally rolling off once he was able to remove himself. I lay on my cot in pain but yet in bliss at the same time.

Columbus I cannot stand. Please dear heart bring me a mug of hot coffee. It will surely take me many hours to recover from what we have just done.

I am sure you will recover Sarah. Every woman I have bedded in the past has said the same as you, but the next day they were always back in the fields gossiping with the other slave women.

I had to know.

Columbus, what are they like.

Who is that Sarah.

The black women. I must admit that I am greatly intrigued by them. They seem so much more womanly than any of the white ladies I have known. Even without any ruffles to increase the shape of their derriere as the white ladies wear the black women still appear to have truly womanly shapes. Is it true? Are they more of a woman than the white ladies?

Hah, you are indeed a silly girl Sarah. All people are different once their clothing is removed, yet in partial answer to your inquiry I will tell you that it is true that the black women I have had the good fortune to bed are more naturally curvaceous than appears to be among the white ladies I have observed. But to ask such a question! Oh lord what fools these mortals be. You amaze me Sarah.

I became bold. I want to meet one of them.

What is that Sarah?

I want to meet one the black women who are encamped on the periphery of our encampment. Will you have one of them come to visit with me? I would truly be grateful to you Columbus. Now come to my cot so I can show you how grateful I can be. He leered at me and took me in his arms before bringing me to the heights of delight as he was so adept at doing.

January 30, 1865

Dear Diary,

Through some manner of persuasion Columbus has brought me a visitor, a comely woman from the black village. She appeared to be in her early twenties but she herself was not sure. The terrible institution of slavery has made the blacks into little more than animals. No records were even kept of their birth. Nevertheless she was of the perfect woman's age to bring men to their knees in desire for her.

We spoke for a while and discussed her tribulations in first her being a slave and now being treated as contraband. She was reluctant to speak at first, being in fear of talking one on one with a white person. However Columbus's presence and his clear speech encouraged her. In a short while she loosened her tongue. I found that she too spoke near perfect English without any of that sad language the slaves had forced onto them by their circumstances.

I am confused Miss Clarkson, why have you brought me here. Are you some sort of anthropologist who wishes to study cultures other than your own? Columbus snorted.

Anthropologist? You foolish girl. Remove your dress. She wants to study you alright. Now out of that dress at once and show miss Clarkson your naked self.

The woman, her name was Deborah, hurried to comply with Columbus's command. She pulled her dress over her head and tossed it to the side.

Standing before me was an intriguing and exciting sight. Deborah's skin was a uniform beautiful deep brown color. Her breasts were large, much larger than my own, comparable perhaps to the women in my nursing corps. Despite their great size they hung in a manner that allowed them to point straight forward from her chest. Oh and her nipples were unlike any I had ever seen or even imagined. Perfectly round large black nipples tipped each of her breasts, practically inviting any person fortunate to see them to take them into their mouth. Her waist was slender. Her body was without a blemish on it.

Turn around Columbus said.

Deborah followed his command so that I was then given the great pleasure of seeing the most perfect bottom on any woman I had ever seen. Each side of the cleavage formed a perfect hemisphere. It was large and prominent, the dream of any man who has ever been with a woman. In sum, she was perfect.

Deborah, I find myself irresistibly attracted to you. You are a wonderfully beautiful woman. Come and sit next to me.

Deborah looked in fear over her shoulder at Columbus.

You have nothing to fear girl. Miss Clarkson is a kind and gentle woman who would never cause injury to even the smallest creature. Now sit as she told you to. No, Don't sit. Sarah, stand up and allow Deborah to undress you. I wish to see both of you next to each other, black and white unclothed together.

Deborah slowly removed my clothing, doing so in such a way as to give Columbus a sensual show. By the time Deborah had me completely without clothing Columbus himself had undressed.

He sat in a rocking chair near the stove, his massive manhood standing in it's full glory. Deborah turned to look at him and put her hand over her mouth when she saw him.

Oh dear. Columbus, you are a giant. One can imagine that Goliath himself from the good book would scarcely reach the same size as you. You must let me take advantage of your great gift.

In time Deborah, in time. For now it is my desire to see you and Sarah holding your bodies against each other. I wish to see the contrast between the black woman and the white woman as they hold each other.

Columbus directed Deborah and I as if he was putting on a play.

Kiss each other. Kiss her breast. Now you suck on her nipples. Rub you hands over her behind. Rub your hands between each others legs as you kiss one another again. Now lie together on the cot and entwine your bodies. Rub your bodies against each other as you kiss some more. Now Deborah lay down on your back and spread wide your legs. That's it, but a little more. Sarah, suck her large dark nipples and then slide down her body until you are between her legs. That's it. Now kiss her down there until you bring her the pleasure that you bring the men in the army. That's good, very good. See how she holds your head to draw you in deeper. Yes she begins to buck her hips against you. See how she moves faster into you. It seems you have found the spot that makes a woman feel so warm and out o control. Hear her moan, hear how her cries grow higher and shorter. You have done it Sarah, you have done it. Feel her body tense as she holds your head tightly between her legs. You have a wonderful skill Sarah it is true.

Columbus, I wish Deborah to do the same to me. Will she let me do you think.

Of course. Sarah lie on your back and open your legs. Make yourself ready for Deborah's love making.

As before we kissed, she sucked my nipples which appeared tiny in comparison to her own, and she slid her luscious brown body along my body until I felt her warm soft tongue on my private area. I was enjoying the feelings that Deborah was giving me greatly when suddenly I felt her body shift and heard her give a deep grunt. Looking up to see what had caused this I saw the cause of this interruption. Due to my dreamlike state I had not noticed Columbus leave his chair and climb onto my cot. He had pulled up Deborah's hips so that she was resting on her knees. With her in that position he had driven his manhood into her with one very long thrust.

Deborah continued to use her tongue on me even as Columbus drove into her from behind. Her tongue began to move in the same motion as the thrusting Columbus was giving her. She let out a series off small squeals with each thrust giving me even more pleasure as she did so. The atmosphere in my cabin was one of an orgiastic party at the most notorious of the New Orleans bawdy houses. The sweat of our bodies, Columbus's manly rumblings, Deborah's small squeals of delight and my own soft moans all filled the air.

Suddenly the atmosphere changed. I felt my pleasure rising as I anticipated my voyage to heaven. Columbus grew stiff as he held his member even deeper inside Deborah. Deborah let out a cry of uncontrolled delight as Columbus filled her.

Just as Deborah cried out her delight I grabbed her head and forced her down between my legs so as to finish her work. I flew from my body, awakening after some minutes to see Columbus still inside Deborah though lying on her back. Deborah was urging him to be slow in removing himself so as not to cause her any harm. When he finally was able to uncouple from her she fell on top of me. We held each other and enjoyed deep passionate kisses as our bodies, slick with sweat, rubbed together. Deborah's large full breasts felt wonderful as they pressed against my bosom.

March 1, 1865

Dear Diary,

The long winter season is over. Though not as bone achingly cold and biting snow as I had lived with in New Jersey, but terrible enough nonetheless. It is good to be able to step outside and feel the sun upon ones skin.

After our first encounter I knew that I needed to keep Deborah nearby. As such I was granted permission to have her as my assistant as I made my rounds. Effectively she would stand guard and hand me the swaddling cloths and tincture of mercury as I either treated the mens personal diseases or the small variety of sprained or broken bones arising from the bored rough behavior of men forced to sit in calm while awaiting excitement and danger.

Of course though Deborah's assistance is merely another ruse. I do not need her nursing assistance. I need her touch upon my flesh, her lips against mine, her soft tight naked body held close to my own.

Columbus has attached our two beds together so that there is room for the three of us during our nightly acts of salacious familiarity. Before I had left New Jersey I had never even conceived of three lovers together. In fact I had barely dreamed of any of the adventures I have had. Yet this arrangement with Deborah Columbus and myself is something new and nearly beyond belief. It almost feel as if I have discovered a new land, just like the real Columbus of yore had discovered the lands west of Europe.

I had been with Robert, it is true, but that was as if I had been with a man. There is absolutely no way in heaven or on Earth that my Deborah could ever pass as a man. I had read that the prehistoric men of ancient times would carve statuettes of the idealized woman for their fertility rites. These statuettes always depicted the women with large breasts and large rounded rears. My Deborah has these same attributes. She is the living embodiment of all that is female in the world. Had she not been black every white man who saw her would throw himself at her feet.

Sadly, because of the terrible prejudices in our society, she remains for all intents and purposes invisible. Yet I find her sensuous beauty to be anything but invisible. The day seems to brighten each time I gaze upon her. I know that it is dangerous, and perhaps that is the appeal, but there are times that I find her so irresistible that I cannot control my behavior and grab her in my arms to steal a kiss from her. At times she herself becomes bold and with a sly smile unbuttons her blouse, telling me that she would greatly enjoy it if I were to kiss her elsewhere, offering her naked breasts to me. I feel so completely naughty when I am with her and it is a wonderful feeling. Columbus knows of Deborah and my secret kisses but does not mind. He calls us his two little harlots telling us at times that we need to be punished. His punishment always takes the form of his filling us with his still unbelievably massive manhood so neither Deborah nor I shy away from our punishment.

April 4, 1865

Dear Diary,

I have received the most dreadful news, almost too much to bear.

For these past three weeks I have been inconsolable. Without the tenderness of my sweet Deborah I fear I would have succumbed to my grief.

I had been discretely making inquiries concerning the health and well being of both Ambrose and Robert. Now that the fighting season is upon us once more I felt it necessary to check on my two brave men. The news I received was terrible beyond all belief.

I have told you of the last time that I had seen Ambrose when he was riding away to raise his mighty sword to smite our foe. He did survive the battle, but did not survive it's aftermath.

Despite being wounded in battle, once he returned to his post guarding the approaches to Washington he was arrested as a deserter! Rather than celebrating his valor as a wounded combatant fighting to preserve our union he was thrown into a military jail to await his trial and sentence. There was a court martial and he was found guilty of abandoning his post in time of war, a most serious offense. Being an officer in the army made the offense even more severe and as a result he was sentenced to be hanged as a deserter.

Alas cruel death had other plans for my brave Ambrose. The wound he received had become infected and while in the military jail he was given the sparest of rations and no medical care. Without proper nourishment or care he died of the flu the night before he was to be hanged. Perhaps posthumously this was for the best, for instead of his death being recorded as the hanging of a criminal it was listed as death by disease. My poor brave man, my Ambrose who taught me so much about how to love a man, died all alone in a dark cell. I can only hope that in his final feverish moments he was given some comfort in thoughts of our time making love together.

As to my Robert I am filled with trepidation. Robert, like so many of the men in the army, had never learned to read or write. It is shameful that public education is so lacking n this country. It seems that learning is largely preserved for the wealthy. I did try to teach Robert some of both, but he was more interested in the affairs of the heart than anything else. Consequently I had not heard from him in a year and could only hope that he would make his way back to me once this horrible war came to its conclusion.

A dreadful rumor has been circulating around the camp which has brought fear into my heart. When one leads a secret life one also runs the risk of the secret being exposed, perhaps with great harm arising as a result. There has been word spreading among the men in whispered tones of a soldier who had been uncovered as a woman in soldiers garb and, once the secret was found, was treated in the most cruel and rough way by her inquisitors as they forced themselves on her. It has been said in words of shame that this poor creature had in fact met her death as a result of her secret being uncovered.

Oh the evil that men do! I do not want to believe that my loving Robert could have been the one to have met such a terrible fate but if nothing else I am realistic in how things often are in the ways of the world. The chance that more than one soldier in our army secretly masquerading as a man despite her female anatomy is slim. I have read of the pirates called Mary Reed and Anne Bonny both oddly encountering each other on the same pirate ship some hundred years ago, but one thinks this is more of a fable than a factual tale.

I pray that I will hear from my Robert once hostilities cease for good. If I do not then I will pray for his soul.

My pain was so great when I heard of the fates of my two men that I took to my bed and would not arise. I had lost all interest in food or personal care, merely lying in a stupor for days on end. Deborah says that I became ill from lack of nourishment and only through her treatment of me as a mother would treat a new born baby was I provided with the assistance I needed to rise from my stuporous state.

Oh my beloved Deborah, who would treat me so with such great love and tenderness. She tells me that she had to chase away all who inquired after me since had my condition been found out I would have been sent north to be treated at a private sanatorium. She says that all the loving nights we had spent together made it impossible to be without me. I too feel this towards her. To be without her would be an end to world itself for me. We share more than just a fleshly bond. We are more like sisters despite outward appearances to the contrary.

My heart swells with love when I think of how she nursed me back to health. I am still in mourning for my Robert and Ambrose, but with Deborah by my side I feel that eventually my mourning will transform into pleasant memories of love long past. The love Deborah has given to me, one woman to another, is what I had secretly dreamed of. To be with another woman in both love and passion is what I feel I will continue to seek for the rest of my days.

April 10, 1865

Dear Diary,

Fighting is renewed. General Lee has made a surprise attack upon our army with little success but still many casualties. His force has been depleted tremendously over the long winter. It seems that General Grant's strategy of starving the foe into submission may have worked.

My nurses and I have work to do in caring for these newly wounded. I do not have my heart in it but I have trained my nurses well and the men do seem happy with their ministrations. I am sick with continual sorrow about the fates of my two lost loves. Though I believed that I would eventually overcome the pain in my heart, with this fresh outbreak of combat I do not know if any amount of nursing will ever relieve my despair.

My dear dear friends Columbus and Deborah do their best to give me succor and I do appreciate their efforts. But dear diary I believe that you are the only one to whom I can truly bare my soul. I must try to overcome my grief and convince myself that only by selflessly giving of myself to our wounded soldiers will I be able to bring myself some peace. If by bringing pleasure to the troops will also give me some degree of happiness then I will be happy to make my rounds.

April 15, 1865

Dear Diary,

It is beyond belief! The war is ended! The southern army has conceded defeat and general Lee has simply gone home. After four years of shocking deadly frightening war things seemed to have

ended with a whimper.

I cannot speak off the fate of our beloved president, felled by an assassin, without tears in my eyes.

But this raises the question: what now?

MAY 20, 1865

Dear Diary,

The last month has been spent sending most of the army home. With no more fighting all that is left is to impose military rule on the south. This requires far fewer troops than the actual fighting had. I have been notified that my services would no longer be needed in the army since there is no longer any front line. Our company's commanding general gave me a few words of praise and thanks before telling me that I had to remove myself from camp within one week.

Columbus, Deborah and I have spent the past several days in almost frenzied love making, unsure whether we would be able to remain together. Although the war is over the status of the former slaves remains in flux.

Last night the three of us spent the night lying in bed and after making love we each discussed our future plans.

Well Sarah, I do believe I will be heading west. There are too many ancient hatreds in the eastern states and I see no future for a black man anywhere from Maine to Florida. I have heard that there is true freedom for all who wish it on the prairie and I have heard there is gold to be found in the rivers of California. Yes, I will try my hand in the wild west as I have heard it called. That will be a man's life for sure. Back here in the east will be a constant reminder of bondage and destruction. Out west I will lead a life of adventure.

Oh Columbus I will miss you so. But you are a strong brave man and I am sure you will have an exciting and adventurous life. Perhaps some day you will write of your life from bondage in Georgia to freedom in the west. It should make for a wonderful biography, almost a work of unbelievable fiction.

Thank you Sarah, but what of you. What are your plans?

I do not know. What is there for a woman in this world. The thought of returning to New Jersey is anathema to me.

Sarah, you have done noble service and brought relief to many an afflicted man. Why not continue your work. Instead of merely showing up at camp and risking rejection why don't you set up an organized nursing corps, not just one for wartime but for all the world. Sadly the history of the world is one of unending ceaseless disaster and calamity. There will always be a need for some persons who will help alleviate the sufferings of this cruel world.

Columbus, you are truly a genius among men. I shall do exactly that. I will create an organization of nurses throughout the land which I will supervise so that where there is a need there shall my nurses be. Thank you Columbus. You have given me a hope which I have found lacking these past few weeks.

And I Sarah? Would you just leave me after all the intimate days and nights we have spent together?

What she said was true. How could I leave her? My heart would break for sure if we were to be separated. I had been with many men in a physical way and with a couple of women as well. I had to make a choice between which way I was to go in my future life. If I were to stay with Deborah I would remain true to her alone. I would be forbearing ever being with another. I enjoyed the embrace of men, their muscular bodies against mine. But they had a rough and dismissive way about them as well. To a man I would b e all but invisible, serving as the bearer of his children and house cleaner and his cook. I could expect the occasional brutish bedtime ministrations that may leave him satisfied but would leave me feeling sweaty and violated and nothing more. It would be a lifetime of drudgery and child rearing. I had had enough of children as a school teacher and wanted nothing more of them. This war had shown me that I had the intelligence and spirit to survive in this cruel world without the aid of any man.

The women I had shared a bed with were the opposite of men. They had a gentle caring touch. They were concerned that I would derive pleasure from our bedding and not just seek their own pleasure. The rough grip of a man did bring a sense of excitement in my body, but only as long as the act lasted. Afterwards I felt alone, almost bereft, as I was simply ignored and abandoned once he had his pleasure. In contrast the softness of a woman's embrace always brought a warm glow through my very being. It was a feeling that lasted long after the act itself. Once our lovemaking ended the women I had been with always held me in their embrace and kissed me softly in loving gratitude for the happiness we had both achieved. I had made my mind up. If Deborah would have me then I would be with her alone, forsaking all others, sharing our lives and our bed together for long as we both shall live. The decision was not completely mine to make though. I loved Deborah, but she had been in bondage and so roughly mistreated by the members of my race that perhaps she would not have me. I had to know.

Deborah, my dear loving Deborah, how could you think such a thing? If you desire we shall travel the country and the world together. But I do not wish to impose my will upon you knowing that you have never had the opportunity to lead a life of freedom. Would you have me Deborah? Would you be my love, my companion through our lives? I do love you dearly and would miss you terribly should we part. If you will have me I will be with you alone, sharing our bed and our lives forever. You bring me such happiness my dear Deborah. Will you be my woman, my lover, my companion for all eternity? If you say no I will understand and with a heavy heart I will leave you to your own destiny. I pray that you will have me though, not just as your companion but as your mate.

Deborah sounded disgusted when she said There is no freedom for women in this country. There is even less for a black woman. Sarah, I have never felt any love or passion for any person, man or woman, in my whole life. I shall be your life mate. Whither thou goest so shall I go.

She pulled me to her and put her arms around my neck, our lips meeting in a long deep loving kiss. She put her tongue past my open lips and rubbed rubbed our tongues against each other in delight. Our breathing grew heavier. Deborah let out a small grunt of pleasure as I ran my hand along her full breast above her chemise. I cold not resist: I undid the buttons off her blouse. Her breast fell out and hung invitingly from her unbuttoned shirt. I gently squeezed it as we continued our kiss. I stroked her nipple until it grew hard in my hand.

Nothing could tear me from your side Sarah. We shall live our lives together in this life and when the time should come in the next one as well. For now however we must repair to your tent. Your lips against mine, your hand on my breast, they have driven me wild with passion. I must have you now.

In my tent Deborah ordered me to undress. I did as she commanded and soon found myself naked before her. She sat on the edge of my cot and drew me to her. I felt her soft full lips suckle both of my breasts. I grew moist between my legs.

Deborah, please take me. I am ready for you. Do what you will with me, but just do it now. I will go mad if you continue to tease me so.

Deborah left out a small chuckle. I shall have you Sarah. Lay down.

Deborah undressed, letting her clothing fall to the floor at her feet. Her lovely curves, her large breasts jutting straight forward from her chest, the perfect roundness of her behind, her soft smooth dark skin all drove me wild with passion. She lay on top of me and kissed me again. I opened my legs for her and she placed herself between them as if she were a man getting ready to place his member into me. Thoughts of Robert and his whalebone device came to me. I had a feeling that this would be a large part of Deborah and my lovemaking. She would treat me as Robert did. I grew excited at the thought.

Soon Deborah was sliding down my body. My hips bucked up as she placed her tongue on my pleasure spot. I barely remember a thing but I do know that my cries of passionate excitement became too loud. Deborah had to place her hand over my mouth so as to prevent our being discovered by those walking outside our place of love. Being held down like this by Deborahs strong grip gave me yet a new and unexplainable feeling of excitement. I liked it. I breathed heavily, my eyes swimming once she was done. She smiled down at me. I loved the way her large breasts pointed down while her dark black nipples rubbed against my chest. I see that you enjoyed yourself dear Sarah. You would not deny me the same pleasure, would you? Come to me, now. Deborah rolled onto her back and spread her legs wide. Kiss me, lick me, rub me until I enjoy the same happy feeling I have just given you. She placed her hands on my shoulders and pushed me down to her womanhood. She gasped. Yes right there, right there. That is the spot I need you to kiss. Do it harder and faster. I soon had her grunting as she held my head in both hands between her legs. After I had brought her to the heights of delight she pulled me up so that I lay in her arms. She held me tightly against her bosom as if I was her child. I could not keep myself from smiling at the feel of her large soft breasts against my cheek. I was aroused at the way she took control of our love making. I was happy.

We will certainly have a lifetime of happiness together Sarah. But why must we wait? We must pack our meager belongings and embark upon our new life, living as a couple as if we were married to one another. We can set up our household together wherever our adventures take us. Let us depart as soon as is possible.

Deborah and I shall leave on the morrow. My dear diary you have been my confidant lo these many years of bloodshed and horror. You have been my confidant in my loves and passion as well. But as I enter my new life as Deborah's mate I feel it is time to bid you adieu. She will be my confidant from this point onward. My future awaits. Goodbye dear diary.

-END-

AFTERWARD

And so ends the remarkable diary of one of the greatest and most renowned personages of the past two hundred years.

History shows that after the Civil War Sarah Clarkson did exactly as the freed slave Columbus advised. In 1866 the Healing Bosom Nursing Society was formed by Sarah Clarkson. As is known to all in the world, this has become the greatest of all disaster relief organizations on Earth far outstripping any others.

Sarah Clarkson lived for another fifty years after the Civil War

ended. At all times she was accompanied by her aide Deborah. It was always written that Sarah and Deborah had a professional and perhaps friendship type of relationship. This diary lays this belief to bed both figuratively and literally.

After the war Sarah and Deborah traveled the world wherever war and disaster arose. They were to be found at the battle fronts of the Franco-Prussian War; The Spanish American War; The Russo-Japanese War; The Philippine War; The Cuban War; The Second Mexican War; World War One and a variety of other lesser conflicts throughout the world in such places as Honduras, Panama, China, and many other far away and exotic places. Everywhere Sarah and Deborah went a chapter of the healing

Bosom Nursing Society was set up. Soon it had become a truly international organization.

Through thorough research of the muster roles of the Army of the Potomac I have uncovered the person whom I believe is the Ambrose mentioned so frequently in the diary. An Ambrose Witherspoon is listed as having died of the flu while under confinement on September 4, 1863. This corresponds with the dates and circumstances as written in the diary.

As to Robert, no mention could be found at all anywhere. But then why should there be? The shock of a woman masquerading as a man in the army combined with her rape and murder is not something that the army would necessarily see fit to publish. It can be assumed that Robert truly did exist despite the lack of the person in any records of the army.

Sarah's lover Rose is likewise anonymous. There were no records of the members of the nursing corps kept by the Army of the Potomac, or of any Army in the war. The nurses were all volunteers and as such had no official standing that could be recorded. This, combined with the general invisibility of women as actual persons and whose sole raison d'etre was to please men, makes it unremarkable that there is no record of her existence.

Sarah Clarkson died on May 17, 1925. Deborah died one week later. As Deborah had said, she and Sarah remained together in both this life and the world thereafter.

And even with the death of Sarah Clarkson her dream of a worldwide nursing organization continued, to this very day. Sarah Clarkson has become like a statue carved in marble over the years. With this remarkable diary it is hoped that her sainted memory will be given a more human aspect for this great and magnificent humanitarian.

CPSIA information can be obtained
at www.ICGtesting.com
Printed in the USA
LVHW080333180820
663477LV00020B/859

PROPERTY OF
FOX RUN AT ORCHARD PARK
One Fox Run Lane
Orchard Park, New York 14127
(716) 662-5001